In seconds, he was up and at the window, gun in hand.

He saw a woman walking down the long lane, headed for the road.

It had to be Hope. Right height, right weight. Same sexy walk. But her hair was short and dark.

He slipped on his jacket and followed, gun in hand.

She stopped when she reached the road. He considered approaching. He should, really. But he knew that if he did, she'd simply lie about what had driven her to leave her warm bed at midnight.

And he'd be no closer to figuring out what made this woman tick.

So he stayed quiet, hidden by the trees. And in less than five minutes, an old car came along. Hope slid in and shut the door. The car drove away, leaving Mack McCann, who rarely got surprised by anything, standing at the side of the road with his mouth hanging open.

STALKED

—

Beverly Long

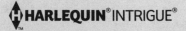
HARLEQUIN® INTRIGUE®

For my mother, who told the very best stories about Colorado.

Recycling programs for this product may not exist in your area.

ISBN-13: 978-0-373-69787-8

STALKED

Copyright © 2014 by Beverly R. Long

Printed in U.S.A.

ABOUT THE AUTHOR

As a child, Beverly Long used to take a flashlight to bed so that she could hide under the covers and read. Once a teenager, more often than not, the books she chose were romance novels. Now she gets to keep the light on as long as she wants, and there's always a romance novel on her nightstand. With both a bachelor's and a master's degree in business and more than twenty years of experience as a human resources director, she now enjoys the opportunity to write her own stories. She considers her books to be a great success if they compel the reader to stay up way past their bedtime.

Beverly loves to hear from readers. Visit www.beverlylong.com, or like her at www.facebook.com/beverlylong.romance.

Books by Beverly Long

HARLEQUIN INTRIGUE
1388—RUNNING FOR HER LIFE
1412—DEADLY FORCE**
1418—SECURE LOCATION**
1436—FOR THE BABY'S SAKE
1472—DEAD BY WEDNESDAY
1513—HUNTED‡
1520—STALKED‡

**The Detectives
‡The Men from Crow Hollow

CAST OF CHARACTERS

Hope Minnow—She's worked hard to cultivate her image as a spoiled rich girl, and she doesn't want Mack McCann to get close enough to learn her secrets. However, she may have trusted the wrong people. Will she pay the ultimate price for that mistake?

Mack McCann—He's willing to play bodyguard for a couple weeks to pay back a favor to an old friend. However, he's not prepared for the real Hope Minnow. Will he be able to save her from a madman determined to seek revenge against her father?

Mavis Jones—She's a trusted friend and employee of the Minnow family. There is a long history between her and Patricia Minnow. Are there secrets that she needs to protect?

Serena Smother—A formerly battered wife, she's trying to rebuild her life. But she needs Hope's help. Will Serena cut ties with her angry husband, or will she lead him to Hope's door?

Wayne Smother—He's been violent in the past. How far will he go this time to punish Hope for helping his soon-to-be ex-wife?

Sasha Roher—She seems to have a good heart, but can she be trusted with Hope's biggest secret?

Patricia Minnow—She's recovering from cancer and pleads with her daughter to accept Mack McCann's protection. Does she know more about the threats than she's saying?

Reverend Archibald Minnow—He's adored and revered by many, but is he so greedy for fame that he'll put Hope's life in danger?

Byron Ferguson—He's a photographer with an almost fanatical interest in the Minnow family. He seems to know more than he should. Is he interested in making news by causing trouble for Hope?

Chapter One

Mack McCann wiped the sweat out of his eyes and reached for his cold beer. He'd been sanding boards in the unusually warm spring sun for what seemed like hours. But he was making progress. The McCann cabin, blown to smithereens seven months prior, would stand again.

It had to be ready for Chandler and Ethan's late June wedding. His sister had insisted that she wanted to be married at Crow Hollow. Ethan hadn't wanted to wait, but he'd agreed because he basically wanted to give the stars and the moon to Chandler.

It was pretty damn amazing that his sister had fallen in love with one of his best friends. He and Ethan Moore, along with Brody Donovan, had spent their formative years at the McCann and Donovan cabins. The three boys had spent summers traipsing around the forests and the lakes set high in the Colorado Rockies, not ever realizing that theirs was a friendship that would span the globe over the next twenty years.

Ethan had enlisted in the army and flew helicopters. Brody had gone to college, then to medical school, then surprised them all when he'd enlisted in the air force. And Mack, well, he'd done exactly what he'd hoped to do since he'd been about seven.

He'd become a spy.

Sort of.

Naval intelligence. He'd worked in more countries than he could remember, and in some of the best and worst conditions known to man. Silk sheets and lavish meals in Qatar, and dirt floors and beans in the Democratic Republic of the Congo.

He'd dined with presidents and princesses. He'd squatted alongside peasants washing their clothes in muddy rivers. His playground was anywhere there was information to be gained.

He'd been working 24/7 for the last sixteen years, and quite frankly, he was tired. And he hadn't been able to shake the feeling that there should be something more. So he'd made the decision to leave.

Of course, he'd cop to having a few moments of doubt over the past months while he waited for his discharge papers to be processed. But once he had fresh mountain air in his lungs, he'd known that coming home was the right decision.

He'd secured a new position as director of security for Matrice Biomedics. The job would keep him in Colorado, close to family. He'd delayed his start date until June 15th, almost six weeks away. Until then, he had few worries. His biggest one at the present time was what to have for lunch.

Fifteen minutes later, Mack was on his second sandwich when he heard the sound of an approaching vehicle. Had his father decided to come early? He wasn't expected until the end of the week. When the car rounded the final bend in the road, Mack shook his head in disbelief.

Bingham Trovell, the man who'd been his commanding officer for a good portion of his career, had his arm hanging out the window, waving like a fool. Mack waited until the car had stopped before approaching. "Has hell frozen over, sir? I can't imagine anything else that would get you on land."

Bing opened his car door and shifted two hundred and fifty pounds of black muscle out of the car. At fifty, he could probably still work circles around men half his age. He'd retired just three years earlier to a little boat and started calling the Mississippi home.

Bing looked at the package of hot dogs and buns that Mack had tossed aside earlier. "Good. I'm glad I made it in time."

Mack laughed and hugged the big man. "Come have a seat at my fire."

It was two hot dogs, two beers and forty minutes later that Bing dropped his bombshell. "I need a favor."

"Anything," Mack said, wiping his mouth with the back of his hand.

"I've got a friend who needs some security for his family. I told him that I knew somebody who could fit the bill perfectly. You."

Mack shook his head. "No."

"Were my sources incorrect? Are you not taking the job at Matrice Biomedics?"

Mack nodded. "I'm securing data and trade secrets and intellectual property. All the things I stole from the enemy. I'm not a bouncer at the front door."

"But you could be a bouncer. You have been a bouncer."

Mack couldn't deny that. His role in naval intelligence had morphed over the years, and there had been times when he'd been charged with ensuring the physical security of important places and important people. "I start working in mid-June. That means I have to have the cabin done by then so that it's ready for Chandler's wedding at the end of June. I promised her."

"We'll get the right people up here to finish the job. At our expense. You don't need to worry about that."

"Who the hell is this person?" Mack asked.

"He's my friend. My old college roommate, actually. Reverend Archibald Minnow."

Mack frowned at his friend. "The television preacher? That Archibald Minnow?"

"Yes. But it's not security for him. It's for his daughter, Hope."

Hope Minnow. Mack had always had the ability to recall information quickly and his three weeks in mountain air hadn't dulled his senses. "She was recently profiled in *People*. Short article. I read it and four others between dress changes."

Bing raised one eyebrow, making his already homely face look even less symmetrical. "Between dress changes?"

Mack waved a hand. "Wedding dresses. Most women want their bridesmaids with them. Not my sister. She wanted them and me." He'd been happy enough to go. There was nothing terribly taxing about being surrounded by four women who smelled wonderful and whose only expectation was a thumbs-up or -down on the dress. Plus, the upscale shopping area where the store was located had recently been targeted by street gangs looking for pockets to pick and purses to snatch.

Call him overprotective. He could take it. But it hadn't been that long ago that his sister had almost died at the hands of their crazy stepmother. Besides, Ethan couldn't go; no way was the groom getting an early peak at the dress. It had to be Mack.

"Well, I hope you found something lovely that fits you well in the hips," Bing said, his tone absolutely serious.

Mack set his gaze on the horizon. "You know," he said, "people get lost in these woods all the time. Their bodies don't get found until years later. By then, of course, all the meat has been eaten off."

Bing gave him a fast, crooked smile. Then he got somber. "Hope Minnow needs you."

"That wasn't my impression from the article. I think she needs her personal shopper, her masseuse and her flavored vodka. The paparazzi caught her at some event in New York City."

"She spends a lot of time there. The Minnows live in New Jersey in a more rural area. It's a forty-minute drive into the city with good traffic."

"Worth doing if you're looking for some action," Mack said.

"She's my godchild," Bing said.

"No offense meant."

"None taken. She was always the sweetest thing growing up. Got married a couple years ago but that didn't work out. After that, she seemed to change."

"Her image doesn't quite fit with the message Archibald Minnow preaches, does it?"

"Not hardly. And I won't defend the man's beliefs but he's been my friend for a long time and I'd like to help him. I definitely don't want anything to happen to Hope."

"What happened to the ex-husband?" Mack asked.

"William Baylor. He still works with Archie in the ministry. There are long ties between the two families. I guess his mother and Patsy Minnow were friends in college."

"Hope must have gone back to her maiden name?"

"Right away."

"It's got to be awkward with him still working with her father," Mack said. "She doesn't work for the ministry, too, does she?"

Bing shook his head. "No. I don't think Hope has anything to do with the ministry or much to do with Archie. He never talks about her."

"Does she work somewhere else or is she strictly a party girl?" Mack thought back to the picture he'd seen in the magazine. Long, sexy legs, short black skirt and a top that showed just enough cleavage to make a grown man beg for more. Pretty face with blond hair hanging down to the middle of her back. Eye candy.

He didn't mind that, but he preferred a little more substance. Although both eye candy and substance had been sadly missing in his life the past few months as he worked feverishly to finish up things before leaving Uncle Sam's employ.

"She used to have a good job working at the Metropolitan Museum of Art in special events. She has a master's degree from New York University. But she left her job when her mother got sick."

Maybe he'd misjudged. There could be plenty of substance there. "How is Mrs. Minnow now?"

"Better. Definitely good enough to travel, she says. Patsy Minnow is a real sweetheart. I've always told Archie that he didn't deserve her. So, what do you think?" Bing prompted.

It wouldn't be the worst assignment he'd ever had. And he owed Bing. Would always owe Bing. "How long?"

"Just for a few weeks until Archie has the opportunity to vet the qualifications of various security firms. He and his wife are scheduled to leave the country the day after tomorrow for ten days and he won't have a chance to address it before then. There's a small group going along, including my wife and me. Otherwise, I'd do it myself. He has to be very careful who he lets into his inner circle. I've vouched for you and that's good enough. He knows

I would never disappoint him and I've told him that you would never knowingly disappoint me."

True. Twelve years ago, Bing had saved Mack from torture and a bad death when Mack had underestimated the enemy. Bing had done it at great risk to himself. That wasn't something a man took lightly. Mack looked around the yard. The cabin was coming along nicely. Somebody else could lay the floor and get the bathroom finished. If he babysat Hope for ten days, there'd still be plenty of time to paint and get the yard cleaned up. There was really no good reason to turn down Bing.

"Okay. I'm in," Mack said.

Chapter Two

Hope watched the seconds tick by on her bedroom clock. Her curtains were open and she could see the sun high in the blue sky. Clouds would likely roll in later, if the weather forecaster on the news was to be believed. They were calling for showers around dinnertime.

She waited another ten minutes, then rolled out of bed, did twenty minutes of yoga, showered and pulled her still-wet hair back into a low ponytail. She dressed casually in black ankle pants and a gauzy royal-blue-and-black shirt. She slipped her feet into her favorite one-inch heels, perfect for walking around the city.

Which she did most afternoons.

Because strolling around New York was like nails on a chalkboard to her father and that made all the effort very worthwhile. Archibald Minnow was embarrassed that his daughter was *without purpose*. That's how he'd described her in a recent magazine article that had come out shortly after the *People* article. She couldn't even remember which magazine because he did so many interviews. Blah, blah, blah. The church this, the church that. He'd have tried to avoid questions about her. But in this instance, they must have pressed and he had to offer up something. *My daughter is a woman without purpose. I pray for her daily and am confident that she will find her way. Now can we talk about the money we need to keep this machine running?*

Although he'd never really say *machine*. Nothing quite so crass. He'd say all the right words. And the money would flow in.

And the cachet of the small-town preacher who had caught the attention of the right people at the right time and made it big on television would continue to grow. Archibald Minnow hadn't been an overnight success but pretty darn close. A meteoric rise, some said. From unknown to household name in just a few years.

And everybody who didn't roll *with him* got rolled over. Most got on board willingly, gleefully, praying for space inside Reverend Minnow's magic bubble.

Hope didn't believe in magic bubbles, and she'd stopped believing in her father a long time ago.

At a very disrespectful and slothful one-fifteen in the afternoon, Hope walked down the curving staircase. When she passed the kitchen, she stuck her head in. Mavis Jones stood at the kitchen sink, washing up a few dishes, likely from the lunch that she and Hope's mother had shared.

"How's Mom?" Hope asked.

"We played five holes of golf today before we took the cart back to the clubhouse. Not bad given that this was the first time we've been out this spring."

"Not bad at all," Hope said. Especially since her mother hadn't felt well enough to play at all last year. Radiation and chemotherapy had robbed her mother of many of the things she loved. It had been a very ugly time. Thank goodness that Mavis, who'd been her mother's friend for over forty years and widowed several years ago, had been there to help. Hope didn't know what they would have done without her.

"Hopefully you'll get a full nine in soon. And the day she walks eighteen holes, I'll dance naked in the street. Or something like that," Hope said, winking at Mavis.

"Me, too. Except who would want to see this old woman and all her sagging and jiggling parts?"

Mavis wasn't kidding anybody. She was still an attractive woman. "You sag and jiggle less than lots of thirty-year-olds," Hope said. "You know that."

The woman shrugged but looked pleased. "You want me to bring you some coffee on the veranda?" she asked.

"I'll get my own coffee," Hope said, walking into the kitchen. "You know you don't have to wait on me." She poured a cup and stuck two pieces of bread into the toaster. Once they popped, she spread the peanut butter on thickly, slapped the pieces together and wrapped her breakfast up in a napkin. "I'll see you later," she said.

When she opened the French doors to the veranda, the warm sun hit her face. Spring had come early this year to the east coast, and flowering shrubs had been in full bloom for weeks. The gardeners had planted annuals in the big urns that flanked the doorway and vines were already starting to trail down the sides.

She walked across the red brick and pulled out a chair. She put her toast and coffee down on the glass-topped table and sat in the sun, facing the heated lap pool that had been opened for the season just the week before. This was normally her favorite time of the day. She loved the solitude. Her father would be working and her mother resting.

But today, her quiet was infringed upon by voices. Men's voices. She stood up, shading her eyes against the glaring sun. Her father was in the yard, well beyond the formal garden area. He wore casual clothes, as if he hadn't yet gone into work. Next to him she recognized Bingham Trovell. Uncle Bing had brought her gifts from all over the world when she was a child. And he'd always had time for a story. To read one, to tell one, to laugh about one.

She didn't recognize the third man. He was dressed the most formally, in dark slacks and a light-colored sports jacket. He was too far away for her to make out his face.

Likely a potential donor. Poor Uncle Bing. Somehow he'd gotten sucked up into the appeal. Her father rarely gave tours of the grounds anymore, so this guy had to have enough bucks to make that happen.

They were walking toward the house. She got up and grabbed her toast and coffee, intending to leave before they saw her.

But her mother stood in the doorway. Still beautiful at 67, the former Miss Texas had put on at least five pounds in the last month. She was still way too thin but Hope was grateful for every ounce.

"Hi," Hope said. "I hear you played golf this morning."

"Yes, it was fabulous. Is that your lunch?"

Hope looked at her toast, still wrapped in the paper napkin. "Brunch. I'm going to eat inside today," she said. She waited for her mom to step aside. But the woman didn't.

Hope looked over her shoulder. The trio was closer. "Excuse me, Mom," she said.

"Do you have a minute?" her mother asked. "Your father and I would like you to meet someone."

"I was on my way out," Hope lied.

"Please."

Hope sighed. She couldn't say no to her mother. "I just have a minute," she hedged.

Her mother nodded and looked past Hope. "Hello, Bing," she said. "You're looking well."

"And you, Patsy." Uncle Bing took the last three steps, leaned in past Hope and kissed her mother's cheek. "You look radiant."

Then Uncle Bing turned to her and hugged her hard. "Good to see you, Hope."

Her father stepped close, in a Prada shirt, khaki shorts and deck shoes. At 67, he still had a full head of hair that he kept brown with some regular help from his hairdresser. He was trim, had all his own teeth and a good smile to show them off.

The camera loved him. And contributions from female fans almost doubled those from males.

As usual, he nodded in Hope's direction but didn't speak. Instead, he pulled out chairs at the table and motioned for them to take one. Her mother sat.

Hope checked out the stranger. Up close, she could tell that his clothes were expensive. He wore them with a casual elegance. His short hair was dark, with just a thread of silver at the temples. He was very tanned, very fit.

She wished he'd take his sunglasses off or that she'd thought to put hers on.

Uncle Bing waved a hand. "Hope, this is my good friend Mack McCann."

She extended her hand. "Mr. McCann," she murmured. When her hand connected to his, she expected his skin to be warm from the sun. But it was cool. There were calluses on his palms and his index finger looked bruised, as if he'd recently hit it with something. Both imperfections were strangely at odds with his otherwise sophisticated presence.

"Ms. Minnow," he replied. His voice was low, sexy.

"Let's get on with it," her father said.

Hope snuck one last look at her mother, who was looking at her expectantly. Expecting what, Hope wasn't sure. She worked hard to hide the animosity she felt for her father from her mother. But she wasn't always successful. Those times she always came out the loser because overt hostility didn't bother her father at all, and it ripped Hope apart when she knew that she'd upset her mom. Stress wasn't good for any recovery.

Hope sat next to her mom and looked at the lap pool. Out of the corner of her eye, she saw her father take a chair. Then Bing, and finally Mack McCann.

Her father leaned forward, his arms on the table. "Bing brought Mack here today because I asked for assistance. Mack provides PPS."

Her father had the most irritating habit of assigning acronyms to things and then acting surprised when other people didn't know them. She didn't rise to the bait. She thought about the water temperature of the pool.

She heard her mother sigh. "Personal protective services, Hope. He's a bodyguard."

Oh, good grief. Her father was going to add a bodyguard to his entourage. That would mean there wouldn't be a seat in the limo for either his hairdresser or his accountant.

She bet the hairdresser got tossed. Or maybe he'd just have the church buy a bigger limo.

"There have been some threats," her father said.

"Threats," she repeated, making sure her tone said *boring*.

Uncle Bing looked at her father. There was no reaction from Mack McCann.

"Threats on *your* life," her father said.

Hope looked at her mother. She could not be falling

for this. But the look on her mother's face said that she'd been reeled in.

"We've hired Mack to protect you," her mother said. "He's your shadow for the next ten days while we're traveling."

Hope pushed her chair back. Took a deep breath, held it. Then she turned to the stranger. "Mr. McCann, I hope you didn't come too far for this appointment because that's time you're never going to get back. I don't need or want a bodyguard." It was the understatement of the year. A bodyguard would ruin everything. Make it impossible to do the things that needed to be done.

She bent down and kissed her mother's cheek. Then she straightened. "I'm going shopping."

THE ONLY SOUND on the veranda after Hope made her departure was the tinkle of water from the frog's mouth at one end of the pool.

"Archie?" Bing asked.

"She doesn't have a choice," Reverend Minnow said, folding his arms across his broad chest.

"She doesn't seem too concerned," Mack said. He'd been prepared for her to be upset, maybe cry a little, or be a little angry that someone would dare to threaten her. He hadn't expected to be dismissed.

"She needs to understand the full impact of the situation," Patricia Minnow said. "I'll talk to her." The woman reached for the papers that Reverend Minnow held folded in his hands.

Mack reached over the frail, yet lovely woman. "I'll do it," he said. When he'd first read the threats, he'd been incensed that Hope was being targeted because someone had a bone to pick with Archibald Minnow. It was damn cowardly to go after someone's child, even if that child was an adult. He'd been grateful that he'd accepted the assignment.

But he wasn't going to guard an uncooperative subject. She had to go along with the plan or all bets were off. He wanted to talk to Hope alone. There'd been some strange dynamic at the table. He hadn't had time yet to figure it out and nobody was tipping their hand.

"May I?" he asked, inclining his head toward the house.

"Of course," said Patricia. "But you better be fast. Hope moves quickly when she wants to."

Mack pushed back his chair. So far, he wasn't overly impressed with Hope's speed or initiative. When he and Bing had arrived at the reverend's house and learned that Hope was still in bed, that she was always in bed until early afternoon, he'd been disgusted. The party girl needed to get her very nice butt home and get to bed at a reasonable time so she could stop wasting her life away. He knew he was probably too much the other extreme, but he was generally up by four, had read a couple newspapers by five, worked out and eaten breakfast before the sun was up.

He entered the air-conditioned house just in time to see Hope, with keys in hand, exit through a door that he assumed led to the garage. He cut through the immense living room, then the study and out the front door just as the garage door went up.

She backed out fast, slowing just a little to close the garage door behind her. Mack didn't miss his opportunity. He opened the passenger door and swung into the still-moving car.

Chapter Three

"Hey!" she yelled.

"A minute of your time," he said. "That's all I'm asking for."

She jammed on the brakes, almost causing him to pitch forward. He could tell that she wanted to tell him to go to hell, but good manners or something had her shoving the car into Park. "You've got sixty seconds."

Now that they were sitting close and there were no competing fragrances from the chemical-rich pool, he could smell just her. The scent was something light, elegant, and it made him think of the rare orchids that his father grew.

Her bare arms were tanned and fit and he suspected that at some point they did more than just lift a martini glass. She probably had a personal trainer on call.

One polished fingernail tapped impatiently on the steering wheel. He glanced at her toes. Yep, they matched. He not only knew his bridal-gown designers now, but he was also pretty up to speed on polish colors, too. There'd been a lengthy discussion over lunch about those. Hope favored something a little hotter, a little sexier, than the pink champagne that his sister and her bridesmaids were wearing.

"You're wasting time," she said.

"I talk fast," he said, and gave her his best friendly smile. It had unarmed bad guys all over the world, but didn't seem to faze her. Her jaw remained stiff. He wished he could see her eyes but she'd put on her sunglasses.

"I guess I really just want to know why you're so damned determined to be careless with your personal safety?"

She pressed her lips together.

He opened the folded papers. "I think you should see these." He handed her the least insulting one. She started to reach for it and stopped.

"You can touch it. These are copies. The police have the originals and the envelopes that they came in. They were hand-addressed and delivered by mail to your father's office. This one came about a week ago." Reverend Minnow had shared that he'd asked Chief Anderson, the local cop in charge, to keep the letters confidential unless there was a specific reason for the information to be shared. Evidently the chief was a devout follower. Reverend Minnow had given Mack the chief's private number and he'd entered it into his phone.

She took the paper. Read it. Her expression didn't change.

That pissed him off. He leaned close and read aloud. "'Dear Reverend Minnow. I lost my son because of you. You need to know the same pain.'"

"This one came just two days ago." He spread the paper out. "'Dear Reverend Minnow. An eye for an eye. My son. Your daughter.'"

She finally looked at him. "I'm not sure what you want me to say?"

"Maybe something like, 'wow, I'm kind of worried.'"

"But I'm not." She took a deep breath. "Do you know that my father has a new book coming out soon?"

Mack nodded.

"My mother's cancer is in remission. Good news, of course. Not great timing for my father. You see, she'd been recently diagnosed when his last book hit the shelves. Gave him the boost he needed for it to hit the *New York Times* list."

Okay. A few things were starting to make sense. First things first. "I'm sorry that your mom was ill." His own mother had died of cancer when he was just a teenager. "And I'm glad that she's getting better."

"Thank you," she said, her voice very soft.

"You really think that your father would engineer something like this just to get some attention?"

"Definitely. Don't underestimate my father. Others have and they've paid the price."

"Bing believes these threats are real."

"Uncle Bing is a wonderful man. But his friendship with my father, which I do not understand, is apparently clouding his judgment."

"What if you're wrong?" Mack asked. "Do you have so little regard for your life that you're willing to take the chance?"

She moved the gearshift to Reverse. "Mr. McCann, you've used up more than your sixty seconds. Get out."

He would have thought she was absolutely as cool as a cucumber, but she had a profound tell. Her pretty hot-pink toes on her left foot were moving. Her foot wasn't tapping. No. Just the toes, expending her nervous energy. If she'd had on shoes or if they'd been seated at a table, he'd never have been the wiser. He opened the door. "Don't be a fool, Hope."

He watched her drive away. Let her get to the end of the block before he moved. Then he ran for his car, which was parked around the corner. Before she got to I-280

East, he'd picked up the car and settled in, staying a discreet three car lengths behind.

He called Bing from the car. "I'm following Hope."

"I'll let her parents know," Bing said and hung up.

She drove competently, staying up with the nonrush-hour traffic. They crossed through the Holland Tunnel and weaved their way through lower Manhattan, then up to midtown. Then she pulled into a parking garage one block off of Fifth Avenue that charged a ridiculous thirty-five dollars per hour. He idled in a no-parking zone, giving her time to get out of her car and down the sidewalk. Then he pulled into the same lot and quickly parked.

This portion of Fifth Avenue was one designer store after another. The shoppers were an eclectic bunch. Parents with children, likely on vacation to the Big Apple, and much more likely, he figured, to be window-shopping rather than buying at the overpriced stores. There were business types—men and women—with briefcases or expensive leather bags on their shoulders and cell phones in their hands. Maybe they shopped but he thought not. Probably en route from one meeting to the next and using the expensive street as a convenient thoroughfare.

And then there were the real shoppers, the people like Hope Minnow, who had the means and the inclination to pay for a designer name and some personalized service. He caught up with her in a small store that was somehow managing to pay their rent selling purses, scarves and shoes.

He stayed outside because the interior was too narrow to provide him any cover. He stood off to the side of the big windows, pulled his cell phone off his belt and pretended to make a call.

He knew there was some chance that he could lose her if she decided to run out the back door but it was a calculated risk. He was confident that she didn't realize she was being followed.

Wedding dresses, nail polish, now the accessories. He could feel his masculinity eroding. He needed some scratching and spitting.

It was a good thing he owed Brody Donovan a call. The two of them were going to throw Ethan a hell of a bachelor party, but first Brody needed to get back into the country. He'd been working on the front lines for a long time, patching up soldiers who had the misfortune to lose limbs to roadside IEDs. The last time Mack had spoken to Brody, just after Chandler had surfaced in Ethan's capable hands, the man was looking forward to getting back to the States. He intended to join the trauma team at one of Southern California's most prestigious hospitals.

The three of them were going to have some fun in Vegas first. Mack had seen the movies. He could do better.

But now, his only real responsibility in life was following a woman intent upon spending her daddy's money.

When she walked out of the store fifteen minutes later, she was carrying just one bag that, by the shape, appeared to be shoes. It made him think of her pretty pink toes again. Shame to cover those up.

She went to three more stores and the pattern pretty much repeated itself. She went in, spent about twenty minutes and came out carrying another bag. Their shapes were not as definitive as the shoe bag, but given the types of stores, he suspected she'd purchased jewelry, dark chocolate and clothing. She was just about to enter a huge toy store when she suddenly detoured from her path and headed toward a bus stop at the corner. There was a group of people but she sought out a woman who was standing with a stroller in front of her and two other young children, one on each side. The woman wore a fast-food worker's uniform. Mack suspected she was either just getting off or just going to work.

He couldn't figure out what Hope had in common with the woman. But it didn't take him long because suddenly Hope was handing the woman all her packages. The woman appeared hesitant to accept them, but Hope must have said something to convince her because she finally accepted the bundle.

He wished he could hear the conversation but he couldn't afford to get any closer. In fact, when Hope turned quickly, retracing her steps, he had to jump behind a group that was waiting for the crosswalk light to come on.

What the hell? She'd spent two hours shopping only to give away the merchandise? He was confident the woman with the children hadn't been expecting to meet Hope.

He followed her as she headed in the direction of her car. They were still two blocks away when she pulled her cell phone out of her purse. She glanced at the phone and answered. Then she walked and talked, an animated conversationalist, shaking her head, even waving an arm. The call continued all the way back to the parking lot and for another ten minutes after Hope was in her car. When she finally put her phone down, she slumped over the steering wheel for a few seconds.

Even from a distance, he could tell that she seemed defeated, and he had the most insane urge to storm the car and demand to know what was wrong. He wanted to fix it. Why, he wasn't sure. She'd snubbed him, kicked him out of her car and made him waste two hours of his life on Fifth Avenue.

But before he could make the decision to show himself, she straightened up, started her car and pulled out of the lot. He got in his own car and followed her back onto the highway, dropping off when she turned the corner to return to her home.

He called Bing again. "She's back, safe and sound. The only thing that was in danger was her wallet."

"I was just about to call you. I'm out to an early dinner with Patsy and Archie before we catch our plane. Patsy called Hope while she was shopping and they had a long conversation. She's agreed to have you provide security."

That explained the phone call.

"Why the change of heart?"

"I could only hear Patsy's side of the conversation. At first, it didn't appear as if Hope was going to give in. But Patsy kept insisting, almost begging her. I guess she finally agreed."

"When is she expecting me?"

"Tonight. But don't expect her to cook you dinner."

He'd be lucky if she didn't throw her dinner at him.

Chapter Four

Hope had just finished her salmon and asparagus when Mack McCann walked up from the backyard. She'd eaten outside because the weather forecasters had been wrong. The rain had held off.

Mack carried an expensive leather bag with a strap over one shoulder and held something else in his hands. When he got closer, she could see it was lightbulbs.

That seemed like an odd thing to pack. He had changed into worn jeans, T-shirt and sandals. He had the job. Obviously no need to dress to impress.

But oddly, he still did impress. It was the confidence he moved with, the assurance that every step he took was exactly the right one.

She envied that. She'd been waffling for months, not able to make a decision about her next steps.

"We have a front door," she said when he got close enough to hear. "Most people use it." She stared at the gun that he holstered at his hip. Of course he was armed. She should have expected it but she'd never been all that fond of guns, especially after her father had demanded that she go with him on a deer-hunting expedition when she was about thirteen.

She shifted her eyes, determined to focus on something else besides the black gun. She frowned at the package of lightbulbs. "You didn't have to bring your own," she said. "We provide them for our guests."

He shrugged. "When your father took Bing and me for a tour this morning, I noticed there were some lights out on the other side of the pool house. Light is one of the simplest and best deterrents to unwelcome activity."

She should probably appreciate his attention to detail. But it was hard to appreciate somebody who was interrupting what would have been ten days of peace. Almost two whole weeks of not pretending to be something that she wasn't. At least while she was in her own home.

"I still think it's ridiculous that you're here," she said.

He nodded and pulled out a chair. He angled it and she realized he did that so he could see both the house and the backyard. He evidently was still buying in to the fact that the threats were real.

"If you think it's so ridiculous, why did you agree to the protection?"

"Because my mother asked me to," she said, blurting out the truth. "She said it was the one thing that I could do to ensure that she enjoyed her trip." She tapped her index nail against the side of her dirty plate. "My mother has wanted to go to Europe for many years. A year ago, when she was so sick that she couldn't even lift her head off her pillow, she had accepted that she was never going to get there. And it broke my heart. Such a simple thing to ask for, but time had run out."

"But she's getting to go after all," he said, "and you're not going to do anything to dull the shine of the experience."

"I love her too much," she said. "And when my parents check in with you, as I'm sure they will, I'd appreciate it if you'd remember that I don't want my mother to have any reason to worry about me. I'll play my part, Mr. McCann. I hope you will, too."

"Mack," he said. "We're going to be living together for the next ten days."

Living together. He made it sound so intimate. And a part of her that had been cold for a very long time heated up, making her almost ache with need.

They would not be alone in the house. "Mavis is my mother's assistant and does some basic cooking and cleaning. About four months ago, she let the lease on her apartment go and moved in here. Right now she's out to dinner with friends, but you should expect her back around nine. It would be good if you didn't shoot her."

She pushed back from the table, making the legs of the wrought-iron chair scrape against the brick patio. "I'm going to my room. Before she left, Mavis told me that the guest room on the second floor is ready for you. Top of the stairs, take a right, third door on the left. There's an attached bath. I like to sleep late. I'd appreciate it if you're quiet in the morning."

He knew where the guest room was. After agreeing to the assignment, he'd reviewed the house's blueprints and examined pictures of the exterior and the grounds, which were extensive. In this exclusive rural area of New Jersey, all the lots were at least ten acres. The trees were mature, providing lots of privacy.

From a security perspective, that could be a good and a bad thing. Good because it wasn't likely that anybody would simply stumble upon the house. That made it easy to separate the good guys from the bad guys. If you weren't an expected guest, you automatically went into the bad-guy column.

Most of the Minnows' neighbors raised horses. They

had barns and fenced-in pastures and horses that sold for thousands of dollars. When Reverend Minnow had walked them around the grounds, Mack had asked about the barn.

"Been empty since we moved in," Reverend Minnow had said. "We're not the horsey type. Hope had a cat for a few years when she was growing up but when it died, I didn't want any more animals around."

Mack would have preferred the barn to be bustling with animals. They, at least, would let him know if someone strange was around. Now the barn was just a large empty structure that provided lots of hiding spaces. That, along with the relative remoteness of the Minnow property, presented some security challenges.

Plus, he had to contend with lots of ground-floor windows and multiple points of access. Hell, even the second floor had direct access—right to Hope's room. There was a lovely little balcony off her bedroom. Only good thing was there wasn't any easy way up to the balcony and the door was hooked up to the security system. However, he'd looked at the specs of the system and he wasn't impressed. It was ridiculously basic and a tenth grader could probably bypass it. And if the alarm were triggered, the responders were from a well-to-do suburban police force that rarely saw any real crime. They wouldn't be much help.

This morning, when he'd been touring the property, he'd debated requesting that Hope take a more secure room in the house. But had ultimately decided it wasn't necessary. If anybody tried to access the balcony, he'd hear the movement and motion outside and have time to respond.

After five minutes, he followed Hope into the house and walked upstairs. He was okay with stashing his stuff in the guest room, but he sure as hell didn't plan to sleep there. He'd sleep downstairs on a couch or in a chair, somewhere where he could easily respond if the home were breached.

It took him just minutes to unpack. He left the room, but instead of going downstairs, he started opening doors. It was one thing to study a blueprint, an entirely different thing to walk through and get a feel for the layout of the rooms.

The big staircase split the upstairs, with two bedrooms and two baths on each side. He and Mavis were sharing a side. When he opened her door, he saw that the bedrooms were laid out much the same, although it was clear that Mavis had a special fondness for giraffes. They were scattered all over the dresser and chest, in all materials and sizes. There was an especially beautiful one in glass and a real ugly one made out of burlap. In the corner, there was a metal one that was tall enough that it looked him in the eye.

He crossed the hallway and checked out the bedroom next to Hope's. It was another guest room and quite frankly, based on the dust that was on the dresser, it hadn't been used recently. He avoided Hope's room, knowing that she wouldn't appreciate him knocking on the door.

Next he went downstairs. Archibald and Patricia Minnow's room was just off the kitchen. The bedroom was spacious, with a king-size bed. There was a separate sitting space, with a desk and several comfortable chairs. Then a huge bath and two walk-in closets, both jammed with clothes.

He glanced into the kitchen, which was painted a nice pale green and had lots of stainless steel. Hope had rinsed her dirty dinner dishes and neatly stacked them in the sink. Somebody had made a loaf of what smelled like banana bread and left it cooling on a rack near the stove.

Other rooms on the first floor were a family room with a wall of books and a big-screen television, a formal living room with overstuffed leather furniture and expensive artwork and, finally, the study. Nice windows, more books on built-in shelves and a desk that he recognized. In the center of the desk was a big Bible. Every week Archibald Minnow recorded his weekly television show from this room. He started and ended the program with his hand on the Bible. Mack had watched a few episodes in preparation of the assignment.

The camera liked Reverend Archibald Minnow. No doubt about it. The man came across as passionate about his faith and committed to his flock. In the segments Mack had watched, Reverend Minnow had spoken lovingly about his wife. He had not mentioned his daughter.

Mack searched the basement next. The house was almost eighty years old and the basement showed it. The walls were big blocks of white stone and the space had not been remodeled or fixed up, like in so many of the newer homes. The floor was cement. There was a treadmill and a weight bench in the largest space. The rest was storage and at the far end, the furnace and water heater.

Confident that he understood the house, he went back upstairs and settled in on the couch. Mavis would return shortly. He'd met the woman earlier in the day, when he and Bing had first arrived. She'd shown them into the living room, where they'd waited until Reverend Minnow had come to get them. Bing had met the woman before and the two of them chatted easily. Mack's impression of Mavis was that she was competent and fiercely loyal to the Minnow family, especially Patricia.

Mack heard a car approach shortly before nine. He

went to the window and pulled back the curtain. Mavis parked her Toyota next to his BMW and came in through the front door. When the alarm went off, the woman entered the code on the keypad to shut it off. Then she reset it.

"Mr. McCann," she said, turning to greet him. "I'm glad to see you. I was hoping Hope wouldn't have a change of heart and run you off."

Mack smiled. "I'm not that easy to shake."

Mavis shrugged. "And Hope Minnow is tougher than she looks." The woman put her foot on the bottom step. "I'm tired so I think I'll turn in right away. What time would you like breakfast, Mr. McCann?"

"It's Mack, please. And don't cook for me. I can take care of myself."

"You sound just like Hope. Looks as if these next ten days are going to be a vacation for me, too. Good night."

Mack watched the older woman walk up the stairs and listened for her room door to open and shut. Then he rechecked the security system to make sure it was on. Finally, he shut off the television and followed her upstairs.

He took a quick shower and pulled his jeans back on. They were comfortable enough to sleep in and he didn't want to get caught with his pants down or off. Then, cognizant that Mavis and Hope were asleep, he very quietly left his room, walked downstairs and stretched out on the couch in the family room.

And he didn't wake up until he heard the very soft beep of the security system being turned off. Then the distinct sound of the front door opening and softly closing.

In seconds, he was up and at the window, gun in hand. He saw a woman walking down the long lane, headed for the road. If he'd been even a second slower, he'd have lost her in the heavy tree line.

What the hell? It had to be Hope. Right height, right weight. Same sexy walk. But her hair was short and dark.

He slipped on his jacket, patted his pocket to make sure that his small flashlight was still there and followed, gun in hand. She was walking fast, her head down, likely watching to make sure she didn't trip.

An ankle injury would put a damper on her escape plans.

Was she running away? That was crazy. He knew she wasn't happy, but running away was for temperamental teens. And she had it made at her dad's house. No real responsibilities. Plenty of funding.

Out for a night on the town? In a disguise? Maybe. But she was dressed in a dark sweatshirt and baggy khaki pants. Not right for the club scene, even in Jersey. And why walk? She had a perfectly good car.

She stopped when she reached the road. She had her arms wrapped around her middle. Her head was no longer down. She was looking to the left, as if she were waiting for someone.

He considered approaching. He should, really.

But he knew that if he did, she'd simply lie about what had driven her to leave her warm bed at midnight.

And he'd be no closer to figuring out what made this woman tick.

So he stayed quiet, hidden by the trees. And in less than five minutes, an old car came along, slowing well before they could have seen Hope. When the car stopped, Hope stepped from the trees and opened the passenger-side door.

The car's interior light came on, showing the driver.

A woman. Dressed in dark blue or black scrubs. Probably ten years older than Hope.

Hope slid in and shut the door. The car drove away, leaving Mack McCann, who rarely got surprised by anything, standing at the side of the road, with his mouth hanging open.

Chapter Five

Hope leaned back against the headrest of the old car and sighed. It had been an emotionally draining day, and while she normally slept for a few hours before Sasha picked her up, she'd been unable to drift off tonight. Because of *him*.

Mack McCann. A necessary precaution, her mother had cajoled. Trusted friend, claimed Uncle Bing.

Brilliant strategy, she suspected, from her father's perspective.

Didn't really much matter what anybody else thought. She pretty much had him pegged as a thorn in her side.

She'd heard him come upstairs after Mavis had gotten home. Had heard the pipes of the old house groan when he'd showered. Could admit that she'd spent a few warm moments imagining how his naked body might look and had told herself it was normal to fantasize a bit, given that she hadn't had sex in almost two years.

And he was seriously handsome with his dark hair and hazel eyes. And physically fit. She knew he'd graduated from the naval academy with honors, spoke several languages fluently and was an expert marksman. Her mother had listed off those attributes this afternoon.

She hadn't been thinking one bit about those things when she'd spent several valuable minutes of her life wondering if he'd packed pajamas in his leather bag. Finally, she'd punched her pillow for the tenth time, closed her eyes tight and thought about the surprise and the delight on the stranger's face earlier that day when the woman realized that Hope intended for her to take all the packages that Hope had managed to accumulate while grazing on Fifth Avenue.

It had been an excellent way to end the day.

"Tired?" Sasha asked, her tone kind.

"No," Hope lied. If anyone had a right to be tired, it was Sasha. She always picked Hope up after she'd finished her three-to-eleven shift at the nursing home. "How was work?"

"Charlie Fenton ran away again tonight. Without his clothes on."

That wasn't a pretty picture. Hope recalled that Mr. Fenton was almost ninety. "Where did you find him this time?"

"Where we always find him. Buying donuts down the street. He was bringing them back for Delores. They're dating."

"That's sweet. How old is Delores?"

"A spry eighty-three. They're talking about getting married."

"You've got to be kidding," Hope said, laughing.

"You would think. Can you imagine?" Sasha gave her a quick sideways look. "Sorry," she added.

Sasha was one of the few who knew the real reason that Hope's brief marriage had crumbled. She'd been there to pick up the pieces. That was how the two women had met. "No problem," Hope said easily. She'd never be able to laugh about her own situation, but she wasn't so jaded that she couldn't feel good about these two old people sneaking around, as much as one could sneak when using a walker, acting like teenagers again.

"Think we'll be busy tonight?" Sasha asked, attempting to change the conversation.

It was a rhetorical question. No one could ever predict what kind of night it would be. The hotline had been quiet for a few nights so maybe it would heat up. They'd had a brand-new client and her two children two nights ago. She'd had two black eyes, a chipped tooth and a broken finger. Her young children had hung on to her the entire night, their little hands tightly clenching her cheap cotton T-shirt. Fortunately, they hadn't had a mark on them, but they'd evidently watched what their father had done to their mom.

Finally, Hope had gotten the four-year-old girl and five-year-old boy to follow her into the old kitchen. She'd convinced them to help her make some cupcakes so that Sasha and Jackie could work with the mom and get her started on rebuilding her life, one that didn't include regularly getting the hell beat out of her.

Sasha pulled her car into the parking lot of the nondescript one-story building. From the outside, it looked quiet enough. Always did. There were no neon signs blinking in these windows. Just a small sign on the door, one you had to be close to in order to read.

Gloria's Path. Named for the founder, Gloria Portland, who'd scraped together grants and private donations to open the ten-bed shelter eight years earlier. Now Gloria worked mostly days, leaving the night work to trusted volunteers and just a few paid staff.

Hope opened her door and got out. As she did, something fluttered to the ground. She bent and picked it up. She leaned into the car, using the interior light to see what it was.

It was a strip of vertical photos of Sasha and a man. "What's this?" she asked, holding the strip up so that Sasha, who was already out of the car, could see.

The woman waved a hand. "Oh, nothing. I went to my cousin's wedding last week and they had a photo booth there with a bunch of props."

When she didn't mention the man, Hope didn't pry. She knew that Sasha had been married and divorced twice. Maybe she was dipping her toes in the dating water again.

Hope gently tossed the strip back onto the passenger seat. "The purple glasses were a nice touch."

"It was that or a felt Santa hat."

The two women walked down the dark sidewalk and Sasha used her key to unlock the back door. The interior was softly lit, in deference to the late hour. But Hope knew that there would be activity. There always was. Previously abused women didn't sleep well. They were worried about their futures, their children's futures. And sometimes it was in the middle of the night that they most needed a supportive shoulder to lean upon.

Hope headed for the small kitchen to grab a cup of coffee. There was a woman sitting at the table. She had a half-empty cup sitting in front of her and she was playing with her smartphone.

Serena was a repeat client, first arriving almost six months ago, shortly after Hope had started her volunteer work. Serena had spent a few days at Gloria's Path, only to return home after her husband had pleaded with her and pledged that he'd do better. When she'd shown up almost two weeks ago, her face bruised and cut, she'd said that she was finally ready to leave her husband, because *better* still regularly included a sharp uppercut to the jaw. She had no children and no other family in the immediate area. By the sounds of it, all she had was a very angry spouse who couldn't accept that his wife of three years had finally had enough.

"I was hoping you'd have a minute to talk," Serena said, suggesting that she'd been waiting for Hope's arrival. "I think I finally have a plan."

Hope smiled. Her night had begun.

MACK SAT IN his quiet car, debating what to do next. The second after he'd watched Hope get into the car, he'd been racing back to the house to get his own vehicle.

Fortunately, his keys had been in his jacket pocket and he'd been on the road fast. He'd caught up with the old Ford three minutes later, two miles outside the city limits of Weatherbie, the affluent commuter community of less than ten thousand in Western Essex County.

Because traffic was almost nonexistent, he'd had to drop back twice to ensure that they didn't realize they were being followed. He'd assumed they were going to roll through town and had almost lost them when they'd turned off the main street. He'd circled back and wasted time looking for them.

He'd found the car three blocks off the main drag, parked next to a square, one-story, frame building with a brick front on the corner of Marsh and Wooten. There was one other car in the small lot. There were narrow sidewalks and a couple of streetlights that provided inadequate illumination of what appeared to be a quiet area. He'd driven around the block once to get the lay of the land, then parked a block away, pulling into an empty spot on the street. He had a good visual of the front door.

During the daytime, there was likely some foot traffic due to the apartment buildings on both sides and a hair salon and an oil change shop across the street. However, in the middle of the night, there was nobody around.

At least not visible. Mack always expected somebody to be hiding in the shadows. It was what had kept him alive to the ripe old age of thirty-eight.

It was the second time in less than twelve hours that he'd chased after Hope. It was starting to be a rather tiresome activity. At least it hadn't been all the way back to New York City. She'd stayed local this time.

But why?

And what the hell was she doing inside the building?

Buying drugs? Possible. But she didn't look like a user. She had beautiful skin, shiny hair, pretty white teeth.

Prostitution? That made his skin crawl. And he felt a surge of jealousy in his gut that he didn't even attempt to analyze.

Gambling? Maybe. She had a lot of money and she didn't seem terribly upset about parting with it.

Dog fighting? He thumped the heel of his hand against his forehead. He was getting ridiculous.

He was just about to get out of his car, knock on the damn door and demand an explanation when an old El Camino with dual exhaust roared down the street. It slowed in front of the building just long enough for the passenger to toss something out of the window. Mack saw the flash.

Holy hell. It was a Molotov cocktail and thrown hard enough that when it hit the front window, it broke through. He could see flames dance upward.

The building was on fire and Hope was inside.

Mack dialed 911 as he raced toward the building. When the operator answered, he reported the fire and indicated the cross streets. Then he described the car

that had fled the scene before he hung up on the operator, who was instructing him to stay on the line.

The front door was locked. He had to kick it twice
before it gave and he was able to push his way through.
The small lobby area was already filling with smoke.
He could see flames climbing the curtains, spreading
onto the small couch, licking their way across the carpet. Heard a woman screaming.

He didn't think it was Hope. That didn't make him
feel any better.

He tried the interior door. Locked. His other option
was going over the waist-high counter that separated the
lobby from a small reception area. He braced his hands
on the counter and easily vaulted the barrier. On the desk
was a fire extinguisher, on its side, as if it had been tossed
there. The pin had been pulled. Mack picked it up and
pressed the handle, but nothing happened.

It was either empty or defective. Didn't matter. It
wasn't helping.

There was another door. This one not locked. It opened
into a long, dimly lit hallway with doors off to both sides.
Women and children, all in their pajamas, were stum-
bling out of those doors, shell-shocked.

Whoever had been screaming had stopped. The
woman who had picked up Hope stood at the end of the
hallway, her back against a partially open exit door, urg-
ing everyone to hurry.

There was no sign of Hope. Where the hell was she?

Then he saw her. She came out of a room, one arm
around a woman who had to be nine months pregnant,
the other holding a sleeping toddler. Her face was pale
against her chin-length auburn wig, but she was calm.

She looked down the hallway as if she were counting

heads and she saw him. Her face registered surprise and something else. Maybe relief?

"Check the rooms," she yelled, not missing a beat.

The hallway was filling with smoke. He used the flashlight on his key chain. It was small but powerful and he could see enough. The rooms were empty. By the time he got to the back door, he realized that Hope had changed places with the other woman. She was bracing the door open and she no longer held the child. He could hear the sounds of approaching emergency vehicles.

Her eyes met his. "I did a quick head count," she said. "I think everyone is out."

"Rooms are empty," he confirmed.

"Thank God." She glanced nervously over her shoulder. The other woman had moved the group to the end of the small parking lot, where they would be out of the firefighters' way.

"I have to get out of here," she said, insistent. "I can't be here when fire and police arrive. Will you help me?"

He had a thousand questions. "What…?"

The look in her pretty eyes stopped him. Fear. Real fear. He didn't know what the hell was up but he wanted her out of there. He wanted her safe.

He grabbed her hand, pulled her around the corner of the building and they raced for his car down the street.

They got inside and she immediately huddled down, as if trying to stay out of sight. He pulled out just as the fire truck rounded the curve.

He drove for three minutes before he couldn't stand it any longer. "What the hell is going on, Hope?"

She straightened up. "Did they see us?" she asked.

He shook his head. "I don't think so. But people inside the building saw you."

"Sasha knows that I got out. I told her I was leaving. She understands. She won't say anything about me being there."

"What about everyone else?"

"I guess I have to hope that the police talk to Sasha. She'll do her best to keep me out of it."

They had reached the main highway. He looked in his rearview mirror. Nobody was following them. "What the hell is that place and what were you doing there? And why are you wearing a wig and dressed like that?"

She didn't answer.

He slowed the car down and flipped on his turn signal, as if he might be turning around.

"Oh, fine," she said, her tone exasperated. "It's a women's shelter. For victims of domestic abuse. I volunteer there. They know me as Paula."

Because he'd had the benefit of seeing the past few minutes, he wasn't as surprised as he might have been. He'd been able to process the scene. But still, her words were pretty damn shocking.

It would have been helpful if Archibald Minnow had mentioned this when he'd given Bing and him the tour of the Minnow estate. "Nobody said anything to me about this," he said.

"Nobody knows," she said. "Well, that's not exactly true. Mavis knows. But she'd never say anything." She paused for a minute. "I assume you somehow managed to follow me."

"Yes." He figured she'd blast him for that. But she simply shook her head in disgust.

"I can't even manage to sneak out of a house."

"Don't beat yourself up. I'm a little more observant than your average houseguest. Who's the woman that picked you up?"

"Sasha. She has a paid position with Gloria's Path. That's the name of the shelter," she added.

"She must know the truth about who you are," he stated.

"She does."

He waited for some additional explanation, but it didn't appear that any was forthcoming. Okay. He'd circle back to that later. "The two of you were doing a good job getting people out of there."

"We got lucky. Sasha was in the reception area when the firebomb or whatever it was came through the window. She tried to use the fire extinguisher but it didn't work. She yelled and I got the person I was with out the door and went back in for more."

That made him feel sick. "You shouldn't have gone back in," he said. "Once you're out of a burning building, you stay out."

She shook her head. "There's no way I would do that," she said simply.

It wasn't said in a boastful way. Just a statement of fact. And he realized that there was much more to Hope Minnow than he had anticipated.

"It was a Molotov cocktail and some guy riding shotgun in an old yellow El Camino threw it through the window. I told the police that when I made the 911 call. That vehicle ring a bell?"

She shook her head. "No. But I imagine the police will want to know if it rings a bell with any of the clients. It's likely someone trying to make trouble for one of them. We work really hard to keep the location of the shelter a secret. It's by referral only and there's no signage on the street. But it is possible that some estranged spouse or significant other got lucky and figured it out."

He turned to look at her. "Maybe somebody was trying to make trouble for you? You're the one receiving the threats."

She shook her head. "I know you don't believe me, but those threats are bogus. Besides, nobody knows that I volunteer there. It's a secret that I've been very careful to keep."

"Something isn't a secret if more than one person knows. You just said that Mavis and Sasha both know."

She shrugged. "I trust Mavis and, well, the same for Sasha. She had a chance to sell me out before when it would have been really bad for me. She didn't take the opportunity then. She won't take it now."

He was starting to get a very bad feeling. "How did you meet Sasha?"

She was quiet for a long time. Finally, she spoke very softly. "She's worked at Gloria's Path for several years. Lucky for me, she was the counselor on duty the night I showed up beaten and broken."

Chapter Six

It was the first time she'd said the words out loud to anyone besides her father. Mack showed no reaction. That made it easier somehow. If he'd looked shocked or surprised in any way that someone like her had been battered, she'd have wanted to kick him.

"Your ex?" he asked, his voice tight.

She nodded. "William Baylor the third. Never met the first and the second seemed like a nice guy. I guess maybe the apple fell pretty far from that tree."

"How badly were you hurt?"

"Broken nose. Fractured jaw. Bruised larynx. He tried to choke me," she added. "Two cracked ribs. Assorted other bumps and bruises."

"I hope to hell you pressed charges," he said, his voice sounding hard.

This is where it got difficult for her. "No, I didn't."

He seemed to consider his next question. "Why not?" he asked finally.

They were pulling into her long driveway. She waited to answer until he'd parked the car and turned it off. "I didn't press charges because I didn't tell anyone except my father. My mother was very ill at the time. We thought she was dying. My father asked me to keep it from her and I ultimately agreed."

There was just enough moonlight coming in through the sunroof that she could tell that he was puzzled about something. She knew what the next question would be.

"Your ex still works in your dad's ministry? What's with that?"

Indeed. What was with that? "That was my father's decision," she said. "You'd have to talk to him about that."

She opened her car door and shut it quietly, even though she desperately wanted to slam it. She didn't want to wake Mavis, regardless of how it made her feel to talk about her father's betrayal. No wonder she never felt compelled to tell anybody about what had happened. When would the hurt stop? Her father had a choice. He could have chosen Hope. Instead, he'd chosen Wills.

And she was never going to forget that.

She unlocked the front door and went inside. She heard Mack follow her in. Heard him set the alarm.

She was going to bed. Going to try to forget the last hour.

"Hope?"

Damn. It had already been a heck of a night. She kept walking. She had her foot on the fourth step when he tried again.

"Please?"

She hadn't expected that. "Yes," she said, without turning around.

"I'm sorry that happened to you. Baylor deserved to have his ass kicked by somebody bigger and stronger."

It was the quiet conviction that was almost her undoing. To fight her own dangerous impulses, she took a deep breath, then another. "It doesn't matter anymore." Then she lifted her foot and kept going until she reached the top of the stairs and walked down the hallway to her room.

DOESN'T MATTER. The hell it didn't. The idea of a man hitting a woman was unconscionable and the fact that Reverend Archibald Minnow kept the abuser within the ministry was absurd.

It was no wonder that Hope detested her father. What was the man thinking? Mack wanted to call him up and demand an answer. Then he wanted to raise some hell with the ex, cause him some serious pain.

Whatever he'd expected when he'd watched Hope get in that car, it certainly hadn't been that she was volunteering at a battered women's shelter. He hadn't expected that she'd run back into a burning building to save someone else. And he certainly hadn't expected that she'd run from the limelight.

Run? Hide was more like it.

And now she was upstairs, doing more of the same. And he was letting her because quite frankly, he wasn't sure what to say to her. *I'm sorry* seemed painfully inadequate. It had been the best he could do.

She'd been quick to again dismiss the possibility that the attack on the shelter had anything to do with her. He wasn't as easily convinced. But there wasn't a lot he could do about it at one in the morning.

Mack sank down on the couch, leaned his head back and closed his eyes. He wondered how badly the building had been damaged. The fire department had responded quickly. No doubt the lobby area was gone, but they likely had kept the fire from spreading far into the main living area. There would be smoke damage but there were companies that could effectively remove that.

Even in the best of circumstances, the clients would need to be relocated to other shelters until repairs could be done. Would Hope want to volunteer at the new location? She needed to understand that there wasn't going to be any more sneaking around. Everything had worked out okay tonight. They might not be so lucky the next time.

He slowed his breathing. Years of living on the edge had taught him the importance of being able to quickly wind down, relax and catch a few hours of sleep. As he drifted off, he wondered which Hope Minnow he was going to encounter in the morning.

When he awoke, exactly three hours later at half past four, the house was quiet. He checked the security system, even though he was confident that it was still intact. Hope had stayed in her room and Mavis was not yet up.

He drank a glass of water. Then he pulled on his running shoes and headed for the treadmill in the basement. He'd always been a runner and preferred running outdoors when he could. In college, he'd been on the cross-country team at the naval academy and had spent countless hours running the track that was across the Severn River. It had wound through a golf course filled with military personnel and politicians who had swings with wicked right hooks.

It was likely where he'd learn the valuable skill of ducking and darting.

Twenty-eight minutes and five miles later, he was feeling much better. He pulled his T-shirt off and used it to wipe the sweat off his face. He wrapped it around his neck, intending to head for the shower.

As he walked up the stairs, he heard the faint sound of a chair scraping across the tile floor. Mavis? Possibly. He silently walked up the rest of the steps and cautiously looked around the corner.

Hope was at the table, sitting cross-legged, with her bare legs tucked under her butt, wearing pajamas that had—yep, those were dolphins on them. She had left her awful wig behind and her long blond hair was loosely pulled back into a low ponytail. Her face was makeup-free. She was reading the newspaper.

She was really very beautiful.

And what the hell was she doing up at five in the morning?

"Hi," he said.

She jumped about a foot and pages flew. And when she landed, she had her hand on her heart. She stared at him and her cheeks got pink.

"Don't ever do that again," she said, bending to gather up the newspaper on the floor.

He caught a glimpse of tanned skin as her pajama top pulled away from her shorts. It made him think that Hope likely spent some time outside by the pool. Her skin was silky smooth and when she straightened up, he had to look away fast.

He walked over to the coffeepot that now had fresh coffee. He made himself busy opening cupboards, looking for exactly the right cup. Damn. He'd been hot when he'd finished his run but he was feeling even warmer now.

Get a grip, he told himself. He was here in the role of bodyguard. "Sorry I scared you," he said. "I didn't expect you to be up." He looked over his shoulder.

"I couldn't sleep." She was fiddling with the handle of her coffee cup.

"Have you talked to your friend Sasha?"

"I did," she said, not looking up. "I sent her a text last night and she called about two hours after we got home."

That meant she'd had almost no sleep. If there were ever a day that she deserved to sleep past noon, today was it.

"What did she have to say?" he asked, turning back to pour that wonderful first cup. He didn't put the pot down. Instead, he carried it over to the table. He filled

Hope's half-empty cup. He returned the pot to the burner, grabbed his cup and took a chair at the other end of the table from Hope.

She evidently wasn't interested in sharing space because she pushed her chair back and walked over to the sink. She stood at the window, looking out, her back to him. "They were able to work out an arrangement with one of the hotels in town. All the clients stayed there last night. They have space for them for the next few days. However, there's a big soccer tournament this weekend and the hotel is booked then. Unfortunately, that means the clients will have to move again."

"Back to Wooten Street?"

Hope shook her head. "Sasha didn't know. Today they will have contractors come in to assess the damage and see how long it will take to repair the lobby and get the smoke out of the rest of the building."

"The police have any idea who did this?" He wished she would turn around. It was disconcerting to talk to her back even though he appreciated the view of her very nicely rounded rear end. No wonder the dolphins looked happy.

"Sasha didn't think so. The investigating officer did ask the clients if they had any knowledge of a yellow El Camino and all of them said no. They could, however, be lying. Battered women sometimes protect the wrong people."

It wasn't only battered women who did that. Over the years, he'd investigated countless situations where, had the truth been told initially, it would have been bad, but definitely not as bad as the cover-up that generally began when one sailor lied to protect another.

"They don't do it to cause a problem," she added, finally turning to face him. She evidently had taken his silence as condemnation.

He held up a hand. "No judgment here. I've learned along the way that the truth is always somewhere in the middle."

She smiled but there was no joy there. "As a child, you are taught to always tell the truth. Then you become an adult and you realize that everyone lies. It's quite a coming-of-age moment." She turned again and dumped her coffee in the sink.

"Not everyone lies," he said, again talking to her back. "And certainly not all the time."

She shrugged. "Maybe not. Perhaps the small corner of the world where I live is just different." She shoved a hand through her hair. "I'm going back to bed."

"You don't have to hide in your room," he said.

She straightened her lovely spine. "I'm not hiding."

"Last night you said that the only person you told was your father. But you also said that Mavis knows. That doesn't match."

She turned to face him. "Mavis knows that I work at the shelter. She doesn't know why. She was cleaning up my room one day and discovered Paula's clothes and wig. She asked about it and I had to tell her something. She thinks that I'm keeping it a secret because I believe my father would use it to his advantage—that he would somehow look even better to the followers if it got out that I was volunteering my time at a women's shelter. She knows that I'm not interested in helping my father build his empire."

"Don't you think she's curious about why you picked Gloria's Path?"

Hope shook her head. "She's never really asked."

Speaking of Mavis, Mack heard the woman coming

down the stairs. She was talking to someone. When she rounded the corner of the kitchen, he could see that she had her cell phone up to her ear. Her hair wasn't combed and her shirt had been misbuttoned so one side was hanging lower than the other.

He took his shirt that was wrapped around his neck, shook it out and pulled it back on.

"I want to come, I do. But I just don't know. I'll have to get back to you. Stay strong, sis. Tell Walt that I'm praying for him." Mavis pushed the end button on her phone.

"What's wrong?" Hope asked, moving close to the older woman.

"My sister's husband in Mobile, Alabama, had a heart attack. He's not doing so well. Their only child died of cancer years ago so Greta's trying to deal with this on her own."

"You have to go be with her," Hope said immediately. "I'll get you a plane ticket for this morning."

Mavis shook her head. Then she walked over to the refrigerator and pulled off the top calendar page. It was one of those where every day had its own page. She crumpled up the paper, opened a cupboard under the sink and tossed the ball into the trash. "I told your mother that I'd be here while she was gone, that I'd watch out for you."

Hope looked exasperated. "*He's* supposed to watch out for me," she said, pointing to Mack.

"Nice of you to acknowledge that," he said. He turned to Mavis. "Look, I've got this under control. You do what you need to do. We'll be fine."

The older woman looked from Hope to Mack and back again. Then she walked back to her calendar and flipped pages. She stopped at one several days in and pointed at a handwritten note. "I'm supposed to volunteer at the library fund-raiser. It's a car wash. They need every volunteer they can get."

"No problem," Hope said. "That's more than a week away. If you're not back by then, I'll take your place. I know how to wash a car."

"You're sure?"

"Sure that I know how to wash a car or sure that I'll volunteer?" Hope asked, her voice teasing.

Mavis just shook her head. "I was going to buy groceries this morning."

"I'm pretty sure that between the two of us, we can handle that," Hope answered.

"I don't have anything baked," Mavis said.

"I make a mean chocolate cake," Mack replied.

Hope raised her eyebrows.

"You wait. You'll be begging for another piece."

Mavis looked between the two of them. "Be kind to each other," she said. She turned to Hope. "You be careful. Don't underestimate the threats."

Hope nodded. "I won't. Now get going. And you may want to take another pass at those buttons," she said, gently wrapping her arm around the woman's shoulder. "I'll help you pack."

The kitchen was strangely quiet after the two women left. Mack sat and drank his coffee. It appeared that he and Hope were going to be playing house for a few days. He'd seen how Hope moderated her actions around Mavis. Last night, she'd been very quiet coming into the house, likely because she hadn't wanted to wake her up. Without Mavis around, all bets were off. The amount of mischief Hope could get into was probably limited only by her imagination.

Great. He better get some new locks for the doors.

Chapter Seven

Hope went downstairs to see off Mavis and then she retreated back to her bedroom for a nap. She didn't see Mack when she was on the first floor, but realized he was outside when, through the open window, she overheard him telling Mavis goodbye.

She didn't care what he was doing. As long as he wasn't bothering her.

She had to admit, he'd been helpful last night. She'd looked up and through the smoke, he'd appeared, like some superhero. And he'd checked every room, saving her from having to go back down the hallway to do it.

Then, she'd heard those police and fire sirens and known that she needed a quick escape. If the newspapers were interested in when she had a drink at some charity event in the city, they'd be all over a story like this.

The whole ugly truth would come out.

Byron Ferguson would drool with delight. The photojournalist had taken an interest in the Minnow family several years ago. Ferguson had been a general nuisance, snapping pictures at events that Hope or her parents attended. He'd partnered up with a writer at the newspaper and they'd done a whole series that had chronicled Reverend Archibald Minnow's rise from small-town preacher to world-wide religious icon. The piece had been good enough to win several awards, although not good enough for a Pulitzer. Still, Hope had anticipated it would rocket Ferguson out of Weatherbie and into the Big Apple.

But Byron Ferguson had stayed in Weatherbie. He'd gotten a new title and she assumed he'd gotten more work. However, he still had time to always be there, every time the Minnows were creating any news.

From her perspective, it was a bit of a love/hate relationship. He'd been helpful several times when she'd decided to give the press a photo opportunity of Hope Minnow, party-girl extraordinaire. She was sure he'd snapped the picture that had run with the *People* article. She wondered how much he'd been paid for that.

If she'd have wanted to tell anyone about getting beaten by her husband, Byron would have been happy to document the damage. It could have been front-page news.

And there had been times—many times, especially in the first few months after the incident—that she'd been tempted to tell the whole story, to expose her ex for the bastard that he was. But she'd given her father her word.

And her father's request wasn't unreasonable. Her mother had reveled in the match that Hope had made with her marriage to William Baylor the third. His family was old money, with a huge apartment near Central Park, an estate in the Hamptons and another one in Vail.

It would have bothered her mother terribly to know that she'd been so wrong about William, that she'd encouraged her daughter to marry a man with a violent temper.

Her mother had been too sick to hear that kind of news. Her father had been right about that.

And as time went by, she became less and less inclined to want to talk about it. Last night had proven that. She'd barely been able to get the words out of her mouth. *My husband beat me.*

It would hurt her mother if she learned the news now. It would cause problems between her parents. There was no way that her mom had rebuilt her strength enough for that kind of strife.

It might cause trouble for her father's ministry and she was okay with that, but once again, that would be hard on her mom. It all came back to that.

She'd keep her secret. Although Mack was right. Once more than one person knew, it was no longer really a secret. She trusted Sasha. Now Mack had the real story. Could she trust him?

She hoped so. He'd surprised her this morning when he'd walked upstairs after working out, looking all hot and sweaty. She'd seen his naked chest and all those muscles and her own body had heated up, all the way to the top of her head.

She'd fought back by standing at the sink, with her back to him. She'd been relieved when Mavis had walked in and he'd put his shirt back on. But truly, it had been a shame to cover up such male beauty. He'd evidently been hitting the treadmill this morning, but she suspected he did more than that to maintain that kind of physical condition.

She lay back on her bed and tried to forget that it was just her and Mack in the big house. The place was plenty big enough for the two of them. There was no need for them to be even in the same room at the same time. They would coexist. Not cohabitate. She closed her eyes, satisfied that she had a plan.

When she awoke several hours later, her stomach was telling her it was lunchtime. She took a quick shower and dried her hair. She pulled on black leggings and a simple black silky T-shirt. Then she carefully assembled her "work" clothes: baggy gray denim pants, a loose lightweight, long-sleeved shirt, tennis shoes and, of course, her wig. She hated the wig. It was hot and itchy but she knew it was absolutely necessary. Thanks to Byron Ferguson, she'd been photographed enough in the last couple of years that her blond hair was likely recognizable to many people in Weatherbie.

Before the fire had started, she and Serena had been in the kitchen, working out the details for Serena's move. The young woman had contacted her mother, who lived out of state. Divorced herself, the mom had limited funds to help Serena get a new start. Still, she'd managed to scrape together several hundred dollars for her daughter. Serena was hoping that money, along with what she'd gotten when she'd pawned the jewelry her husband had given her, would be enough to rent a small apartment in Weatherbie.

Hope wasn't so sure. While the rent there didn't begin to compare with the rent that someone would pay in New York City, it still wasn't cheap.

As Hope gathered up her work clothes, by habit she reached for her leather satchel that she always used to carry them. She stopped, hand in midair, realizing that she didn't need to hide the items. In the past, she would leave the house as Hope Minnow, stop at the convenience store two miles down the road, use the ladies' restroom to change and emerge as Paula.

It was rather liberating to realize that, for the first time ever, she'd be able to walk out of her room and not have to hide Paula, whom she rather liked. At least she liked her a whole lot better than Hope, who was drifting these days, caught in a place where she'd let her old life go, but she hadn't yet fully embraced a new path.

Hope acted upon her aggression toward her father by spending his money and getting photographed in situations that he might find uncomfortable or at odds with his public persona.

Her master's degree wasn't in psychology, but that didn't mean that she didn't understand what she was doing. She acted out in a rather classically passive-aggressive way toward her father. Because she was angry at him. *Very, very angry,* to coin a phrase from Richard Gere in *Pretty Woman*. She loved that scene. He and Julia Roberts were in the bathtub and after he admitted that he was very angry with his father, she wrapped her legs around him, citing some amazing fact that her legs were forty-four inches long so that she could offer eighty-eight inches of therapy.

She couldn't help but wonder how long Mack's legs might be.

Good grief. She needed *real* therapy.

She pulled her pants and shirt on over her leggings and T-shirt. She put the shoes on. She pulled Paula's cell phone out of the leather bag where she always kept it. Then she walked down the big staircase, carrying her wig and the phone. She could smell bacon. When she got to the kitchen, she stopped in the doorway. Mack stood behind the counter, a cutting board in front of him. He was slicing tomatoes. There was already a stack of lettuce leaves on a plate.

"Hello, Paula," he said. "Sleep well?"

The fact that he'd so clearly grasped that she wasn't just pretending to be someone different, but that she really was someone different when she pulled on Paula's clothes, struck her hard.

"Pretty well," she said.

"New outfit?" he asked.

"Even Paula can't wear khaki pants every day," she said, smiling.

"New phone?" he asked, looking at the simple flip phone.

"Hope has a smartphone," she said. "I buy a prepaid phone at the drugstore and that's what Paula uses."

"You're pretty good at this double life," he said.

"Good enough," she agreed. She'd been doing it for eight months and nobody had caught on yet. "I noticed that my other clothes reek of smoke. I'm going to put them in the wash." She hesitated. "I could throw your jeans from last night in, too, if you'd like."

"No need. Already did a load this morning when you were sleeping. Hope you like BLTs," he said, as if it were the most natural thing in the world for him to make her a sandwich. "I cut up some fruit, too," he said, pointing to a bowl on the counter.

She was truly flabbergasted. Her bodyguard also did laundry and cooked. "How much is my father paying you?"

The minute she said it, she was sorry. It sounded so bitchy. "I certainly didn't expect this," she added, trying to soften the harshness of her earlier words.

"We have to eat. I shine at breakfast, can muddle my way through lunch and if you like steak, I'm good for dinner, too. But Mavis was right. We need to make a grocery run. Maybe we could do that this afternoon?"

Her stomach growled. Loudly. She pulled a plate out of the cupboard and started building her sandwich. Ten minutes later, halfway through lunch, she put down her fork. "This is really good. Thank you."

"You're welcome," he said. He stared pointedly at the wig that she'd placed at the end of the counter. "What are your plans for the day, Paula?"

She took a drink of water. Then a second one.

He waited patiently, as if he had all day.

"There's a woman who needs to find an apartment. She's been at the shelter close to the maximum time that she can stay there. I told her that I'd help her look this afternoon."

He nodded. "In Weatherbie?"

"Yes. While she might prefer leaving, she has a good job in town as an occupational-therapy assistant and she doesn't want to leave it."

"What's her story?"

"Dated her high-school sweetheart for several years. They were going to get married. But before that could happen, he got blown up by a roadside bomb in Afghanistan. Six months later, a friend introduced her to Wayne. They dated for about six months before they got married. He hit her for the first time on their second anniversary. He was upset that they hadn't yet managed to get pregnant. Evidently, he's big on children."

"So, she left him?"

"Not right away. She actually first sought help from Gloria's Path about six months ago. However, he promised to be good and she so desperately wanted to believe him."

"She still loved him after that?" Mack asked, his tone disbelieving.

"Maybe. And maybe it was just hard for her to admit publicly that she made a big mistake by choosing him. Anyway, it took a couple more trips to the emergency room before she finally decided that she'd had enough. That's when she came to Gloria's Path a second time."

"She tell the police?"

"Yes. This time. And he was arrested. Spent a night in jail before he bonded out. He's not very happy with her."

"What's Wayne's last name?"

"Smother. Wayne Smother."

He raised an eyebrow. "Smother? Really? He doesn't walk around with a pillow, does he?"

She smiled. "I know. It's a ridiculous name. But really, who am I to talk? Minnow?"

"Bet that was fun in middle school."

She nodded. "Minnow became Catfish, Guppy, Goldfish because of my hair, and then there was the perennial favorite, when they messed with both my first and last names, and I became Hopeless Fish Bait."

"Hopeless Fish Bait," he repeated. "I like it. Sounds like a rock band from the nineties."

"Lovely." With a smile, she pushed her plate away and stood up. "I'll only be gone for a few hours. I can stop at the store on my way home."

"Where you go, I go," he said, taking a big bite of his sandwich. He chewed.

"That's impossible," she said. "Listen, it's the middle of the day. Broad daylight. Nothing is going to happen to me."

"You're right. Nothing is going to happen to you." He used his napkin to wipe off his mouth.

"How am I going to explain you?" she asked, her voice rising. "Paula doesn't have a bodyguard."

He shrugged, looking unconcerned. "Pick another *B*."

"What?"

"Brother, boyfriend, babysitter, butler, banker—"

"Stop. You're being ridiculous."

"No, ridiculous is being careless with your personal safety. Your father, mother, Bing and Mavis all think that the threats are legit. That's good enough for me. I'm your shadow. Now that you've been fed, are you willing to listen to the rules?"

"Rules?" She raised an eyebrow.

"Yeah, rules. Rule number one—don't go anywhere without telling me where you're going. Rule number two—when I tell you to do something, do it right away, no questions asked. For example, if I say get down, then hit the dirt. Don't debate me."

"I recall Uncle Bing mentioning that you'd been in the navy. You must have been in charge." She made sure he understood that it wasn't a compliment.

He put his chin in the air. "Think I'm bossy, huh? I come by it naturally. I have a younger sister."

She hadn't thought about him having family. He wasn't wearing a ring so she didn't think he was married. Plus, what wife would let her husband play bodyguard to another woman?

"How old is your sister?"

"Almost thirty. Eight years younger than me. She's getting married this summer. I guess she's old enough."

For sure. "I was thirty when I got married. Divorced at thirty-two. I hope she has better luck."

"She's marrying a great guy. One of the best."

"Good for her." She figured she might as well ask. "How about you? Are you married, Mack?"

"Nope. I haven't been in one spot long enough in the last sixteen years to get married."

"But now you're done with the military?"

"Yeah. I'm going to put down some roots in Colorado. That's where my sister and my dad live."

"Are your parents divorced?"

"My mom died when I was in high school. Cancer."

The most awful *C* word in the world. "I'm sorry," she said, swallowing hard. "I was older when my mother got sick and it was still so very hard. I can't imagine what it was like for you in high school. And for your sister. She was just a little girl when she lost her mother. And how sad for your dad."

He looked away and for once, she caught just a hint of vulnerability on his handsome face. "It was hard on the whole family. My mom was pretty special. My dad didn't remarry for twenty years and then when he did, his new wife turned out to be a traitor. Six months ago, after she tried to kill my sister, she was arrested for attempted murder and treason. She's going to be in prison for a long time."

Wow. And she'd thought her life had some drama. She pushed her hair back behind her ears. The silence in the room was deafening. "Have you guys thought about becoming a reality-television show?"

It was a little irreverent but it broke the tension immediately. He winked at her. "Want to make a guest-star appearance?"

"Maybe sometime," she said. "Paula doesn't have a bodyguard or a butler or a banker. But she could have a brother. And that appears to be a role you could convincingly play. Let's go. Serena will be waiting for me."

Chapter Eight

They were halfway to town before Hope spoke again. "Serena's not too keen on men right now."

He glanced sideways at her. She had left off her wig for the ride to town, thank goodness. It rested in her lap like a fox fur. "I imagine not," he said. He waited a minute. "So, are you my younger or older sister?"

She gave him a dirty look. "Younger. Much. We have very little in common."

"What's your favorite color?"

"Why?"

"I think I'd know that about you. That would have been the used-up color in your crayon box."

"Yellow." She paused. "You?"

"Men don't have favorite colors. And if I'm much older, then my crayons would have disappeared long before you came along."

She considered that. "Favorite food?"

"Chicken enchiladas. Spicy."

"I thought you said that the only dinner you could make was a mean steak?"

"I don't have to be able to make it myself to love it. Best enchilada maker was aboard the *USS Higgins*. I was on ship for several months and I never got tired of enchilada night."

"I thought you were an intelligence officer. Did you actually spend time on board a ship?"

"Absolutely. At different times, in different places. Sometimes my stays were as short as a couple hours, sometimes as long as a couple months. Sometimes the ship was in port and sometimes, at sea."

"I assume an intelligence officer gathers intelligence. Right?"

"Gathers. Analyzes. Tries to figure out what's real and what's been leaked to keep you chasing your tail. After 9/11, there was data overload. Somebody had to figure out what was important and connect the dots between pieces of information gathered from all over the world."

"And that somebody was you?"

"I was always good at puzzles."

They were at the edge of town. Hope pulled on her wig and even though he'd expected it, he was still startled by her change in appearance. It was no wonder she'd been successful at keeping from being recognized. Unless somebody looked past the ugly clothes and dull hair, they would never realize it was Hope Minnow, all dressed down.

But she wouldn't have had to have been recognized. Two people knew her secret. Her friend Sasha and Mavis. If they had each told two people who had each told two people, the math became exponentially dangerous.

They entered the unimpressive lobby of the chain motel and passed by the reservation desk. Hope punched the elevator button. She'd gotten the room number from Sasha. On the third floor, they got out and knocked on 310. "Remember," Hope stressed, "it's Paula."

"This is not my first time at the dance," he said, somewhat irritated that she'd underestimated his ability to quickly go undercover. Hell, for six months in Af-

ghanistan he'd been someone very different than Mack
McCann, and the information he'd managed to gain had
been very valuable.

A woman, mid-twenties, with some crazy railroad-
track tattoo on her neck, opened the door. She smiled at
Paula and then her gaze shifted to him. Her eyes turned
wary.

He smiled and tried to look harmless.

"Serena, this is my brother, Mack. He's visiting from
out of town. I told him he could come along today."

Mack considered extending his arm for a handshake
but decided to let her make the first move. All he got
was a nod.

"Ready?" Hope asked.

"I got a text from Wayne," Serena said.

"And?" Hope prompted.

"He said that he'll go for counseling."

"Do you believe him?" Hope replied, her tone neutral.

"I believe that he believes he will. But when it comes
right down to it, he won't go. Just like before."

"Did you answer the text?"

"I told him I was getting an apartment. Not where,
of course."

Mack doubted there were all that many apartments in
the pricy suburb. Lots of estates like the Minnows' and
probably some nice condos, too. The rental market was
probably not so great. Renters were expected to move
along to the cheaper suburbs.

"All right," Hope said.

He got the impression that she wasn't thrilled that Serena had communicated with her estranged husband. But
perhaps she'd expected it.

"We'd better get going," Hope said.

They were barely in the car before Serena leaned forward from the backseat, as if she were a little kid excited about going on a journey. "Thank you, Paula," she said. "I know I should be able to do this by myself but I just feel so much better having you here."

"I'm happy I can help," Hope said.

She was, he thought. He keyed in the address that Serena read off to him into his GPS. The apartment was less than three miles from the hotel.

"I didn't know you had a brother," Serena said. "You never mentioned that."

"Mack and I don't see that much of each other," Hope said easily.

"What do you do for a living, Mack?" Serena asked.

"Just got out of the navy," he said. It was always best to stick as close to the truth as possible, even when one was lying.

"Wayne was in the navy, too," Serena said. "Before we were married. He didn't talk about it much. I don't think he liked it."

"Military service isn't for everyone," Mack said. True. But maybe Wayne, who apparently had an anger management problem, hadn't been able to abide by the rules that were necessary to keep the military running smoothly.

The apartment building was a three-story brick-and-frame combination, circa 1970, with nice square windows and a roof that looked recently patched. There were sliding glass doors that led to small balconies on both the second and third floors. The parking lot next to the building was empty with the exception of two cars. Likely most everybody was working during the middle of the day. The trees around the building were mature and the grass needed to be mowed. It was close enough to the train station that renters could easily catch a train into the city for work or play.

All in all, it looked as if it might suit a young woman looking for a fresh start.

"I hope I can afford this," Serena said.

"Let's see the inside before you start worrying about money," Hope said.

The three of them got out of the car and walked inside. The landlord, a man of almost sixty with a slight limp, met them in the lobby, and led them up the staircase. When he unlocked the door of the second-floor apartment, Serena was the first inside. It took her just a few minutes to look in both bedrooms and the bathroom, and then return to the space that served as both kitchen and living room. She stood still for just seconds before she pulled open the vertical blinds that evidently came with the apartment and opened the sliding glass door. The balcony was probably only three-by-two, barely large enough for a couple of lawn chairs. She stepped outside and looked over the railing.

A princess surveying her new kingdom.

A survivor grateful for another day.

She came back inside, carefully locking the door behind her. She seemed less agitated than before, as if she'd come to a decision.

"What do you think?" the landlord asked.

It was okay, Mack thought. Lots of white walls and beige carpet. But it was better than living on the street or in a women's shelter. Much better than living with somebody who used you as a punching bag. Evidently Serena was thinking the same thing because she was nodding her head.

"I think it could work," she said. "How much?"

"First and last month's rent plus a security deposit of 800 dollars. Total of 2,400 dollars."

The woman's face fell. "I didn't think about the security deposit. I should have. I just don't have that much."

Mack was about to step up and offer to cover the deposit but Hope beat him to it. "May we have a minute?" she said to the landlord.

"Sure." He walked out into the hallway, leaving the door open a crack.

"Do you like it?" Hope asked.

"I do. And the train is so close, I wouldn't need to buy a car to get to work. But I don't have that much cash. I could probably cover the first and last month's rent if I didn't eat much for a couple weeks, but the security deposit makes it way too much."

"We have some funds available through the shelter. How about we cover the security deposit plus we'll advance you a couple hundred to cover food and other expenses until you get your first paycheck?"

Serena's eyes filled with tears. "Really? Gloria's Path would do that?"

Gloria's Path wasn't writing any checks. Mack was confident of that. Hope Minnow was going to fund this woman's escape on her own dime. He figured it wasn't the first time.

"Absolutely," Hope said. She opened the door and motioned the landlord back inside. He produced a lease, Hope and Serena read it and then Serena signed on the dotted line.

"I'll need the money before I turn over any keys," the landlord said.

"She'll be back tomorrow," Hope said. "At noon."

Serena practically skipped back to the car and Mack realized that a heavy weight had been lifted from the woman's shoulders.

He drove back to the hotel and they dropped off Serena. Once it was just the two of them in the car, he turned to Hope. "You do that often? Give money to the clients?"

"Who said I was giving her money?" Hope asked innocently.

"I did."

She shrugged. "It's no big deal. She needs it and I have it. The important thing is making sure that no woman ever goes back to her abusive spouse simply because she doesn't have the financial resources to live on her own." She pulled off her red wig and shook out her long blond hair.

Mack desperately wanted to run his fingers through it. Instead, he kept his hands tightly clenched around the steering wheel.

Then she took off her shirt and her baggy pants.

She had black leggings and a black T-shirt underneath. He hadn't realized that when she'd started ripping off her clothes.

"We need to buy groceries," he said. See, he could act normal even when his heart was skipping every other beat.

"Turn left at the next corner," she said. "There's a store two blocks down on the right. I can run in."

"Where you go, I go," he reminded her, proud that his voice didn't crack. She had no idea how gorgeous she was.

She rolled her eyes. Even that was cute.

"People in Weatherbie know that I don't have a brother," she said.

"There are *B*'s left," he said, reminding her of their earlier conversation. "If none of them suit you, work your way to the *C*'s."

"I have one. How about Crazy?"

"Works for me. I'll be your Crazy Cousin Charlie."

She held up a hand. "Stop. I have to live here long after you've forgotten my name. Let's just go inside, buy some groceries like normal people and if anybody asks, I'll tell them that you're a friend visiting from out of town. Just don't strike up a conversation with anybody."

Chapter Nine

"Do you shop here regularly?" he asked as they walked from the car into the store.

She shook her head. "No. But Weatherbie is a small town. I'm bound to know somebody here."

It didn't take him long to realize that regardless of whether Hope knew anybody, she was *known*.

There was one woman checking out groceries with a man bagging. Both looked up, glanced at him and then settled their gazes on Hope. Then they looked at each other.

Hope ignored them and pulled a cart from the rack. She proceeded to load it up with fresh fruits and vegetables, some chicken, fish, whole-wheat pasta and freshly made marinara sauce from the in-store kitchen. He threw in two nice-looking steaks and some baked potatoes. When he realized she was going to pass up the chip aisle, he grabbed several bags and a jar of salsa. She frowned at them. He ignored her and picked up a gallon of ice cream.

"I would not have expected you to eat junk," she said.

"I eat all the basic food groups," he said, throwing in a bag of red licorice. "It's just that I've spent some time in places where you can't get ice cream or candy or many of the things that make life worth living. When

I can get my hands on something I like, I don't pass up the opportunity."

She hit the cleaning-products aisle and started grabbing things right and left. There was practically no room left in the cart when she finished.

"Your house doesn't look dirty," he said.

"It's for Serena. Cleaning products are expensive. She's not going to have a lot of extra money for things like this."

Would she ever stop surprising him?

They rounded the end of the last aisle and she stopped so suddenly that he almost rammed into her.

"Damn," she groaned. "I have the worst luck."

He looked over her shoulder. A man was walking toward them. Mack recognized him from the pictures that he'd studied.

William Baylor. Hope's abusive ex-husband.

Mack stepped in front of Hope. *Give me a reason, Baylor. Give me a reason.*

"Don't make a scene," Hope hissed and grabbed his arm.

"Hello, Hope," Baylor said, his tone conveying his own surprise. "I didn't know you shopped here."

Hope glanced at the front of the store. The two clerks were staring back. "In the area," she said quickly, likely trying to follow her own advice not to attract too much attention. "Excuse us. We're in a hurry."

Did Baylor know who he really was? Archibald Minnow had sworn that there were only seven people who knew about the threats—himself, his wife, Hope, Mavis, Bing, Chief Anderson and Mack.

Had he conveniently forgotten to mention that he'd told William Baylor? Mack didn't think so given the way Baylor was looking him over.

"I don't think we've met," Baylor said. "I'm William Baylor, Hope's ex-husband." He extended his arm to shake.

Before Mack could speak, Hope stepped forward. "This is Mack McCann, my boyfriend."

Boyfriend. She'd gone with a *B* word after all.

And, hell's bells, was that her arm wrapping itself around his waist? He kept his face neutral.

Baylor's face, however, was getting red. "I didn't realize you were dating anyone," he said, as if he had a right to know.

Mack wrapped his own arm around Hope's shoulders and pulled her close. "I think we're a little past dating," he said. He brushed a kiss across her forehead and to her credit, she didn't pull back.

"Honey, I'm starving," he said. "Let's go home and get these steaks on the grill."

With one arm still around Hope, he used his other to push the cart around Baylor. He could see that both cashiers were still looking at them. He knew a little about small towns, having spent some time in them over the years. Word was going to spread that Hope Minnow had herself a boyfriend.

They checked out and he pushed the grocery cart to the car. Hope helped him load the groceries without saying anything. She got in and sort of collapsed down onto the seat.

"I'm sorry," she said, after a long moment of silence.

"What for?" he asked.

She looked at him as if he was losing his mind. "For using you. I just didn't expect to see him. I wasn't prepared. He's such a smug bastard."

"Just forget him," Mack said. He started the car and pulled out of the lot.

"He likes to pretend that our marriage didn't work because I was too young, too flighty. If I'd worked harder at it, we would have made it. That's the story he tells himself. And anybody else who will listen."

He kept quiet. She was on a roll.

"I had this crazy need to one-up him. To prove that I was moving on. You...you were convenient."

That hurt a little. "Don't beat yourself up." He drove a little farther. "You know, I got the general impression that William Baylor the third isn't necessarily over you."

"Well, I'm done with him," she said, her tone adamant.

"And you're sure he doesn't know anything about you volunteering at Gloria's Path?"

She shook her head. "If he knew, then my father would know. And I'd have heard about that, trust me."

Trust me. Strangely enough, he did. A day ago, he'd have bet his last nickel that he could trust Hope Minnow about as far as he could throw her. But the Hope Minnow that the world knew was the very tip of the iceberg. Under the water was a whole other person. Somebody interesting. Somebody he liked. Respected.

"How do you like your steak?" he asked.

She grabbed the change of topic as if it were a lifeline. "Medium rare. And I don't bother with baked potatoes unless there is sour cream."

"Understood. I'll cook tonight. You can have tomorrow."

"Fair enough," she said.

He pulled into the long lane and drove the quarter mile up to the house. When Hope reached for her door handle, he said, "I'll go first. I'll come back for the groceries once I check the house."

She reached for her purse, pulled out an emery board and starting filing her nails. He got the message. He could act as if the threat were real. She, in turn, was going to make her point that he was nuttier than a squirrel because it was all some bogus publicity stunt dreamed up by her father.

He got out of the car, locking the doors behind him. He walked up the steps, unlocked the front door and was happy to hear the security-system alarm. He keyed in the code and looked around. The rug near the door was slightly off-center, just as he'd left it. The center desk drawer was open an inch. He'd done that right before they'd left. He turned the handle of the basement door. Locked. Just the way it should be.

He ran upstairs, gave it a quick run-through, and when he was happy it was secure, he went downstairs and back outside.

And realized the car was empty.

Using the house to protect this back, he pulled his gun, raised his arm to shoulder height and rotated in a semicircle. There was no sign of her.

He glanced at the brick driveway. It offered no clues.

He left the relative safety of the porch and ran to the passenger-side door. He glanced inside. No sign of struggle. Her purse was still on the floor. The emery board had been tossed on the gearshift console that separated the two front seats.

With the car at his back, he looked around. He'd been gone less than a minute. Even if someone had been waiting for them, they could not have taken her far.

He stood perfectly still, listening. No car, either approaching or leaving. No barking dogs. Nothing unusual at all.

Except that there was a flock of sparrows near the door of what would have been the horse barn if the Minnows had been the horsey type, swooping and diving, as if they'd recently been disturbed.

He ran toward the building and pulled open the door. It was dark inside and musty-smelling. He waited for his eyes to adjust, then eased around the corner.

And there was Hope.

Chapter Ten

Hope was sitting on the cement floor, holding a white cat that was as big as a midsize dog.

Well, maybe not really, but his perception was a bit off because he was damn happy to see her and damn angry that she hadn't stayed in the car.

"What the hell are you doing?" he said.

Her head jerked up and she must have tightened her arms because the cat, sensing a change, shifted its big body and squirmed away. He ran and slipped under the lower rung of a wooden gate that led deeper into the big barn.

"Fred!" Hope called.

Fred evidently didn't intend to stick around for introductions. Hope got up from the dirty cement floor and dusted off her butt.

And damn him, he couldn't take his eyes off the motion.

"I told you to stay in the car," he said.

"I'm sorry," she said. "I saw Fred come around the corner of the barn and squeeze through the door. I haven't seen him for weeks."

He remembered the reverend's comments about Hope having a cat at one time. "I thought there were no animals," he said.

"Fred belongs to the Websters. They have the place next door. He spends a lot of time here. Probably because I feed him," she admitted. "Now be quiet."

She pointed to a place behind a wooden gate that might have at one time penned in horses or cattle. Now, there was one orange tabby cat and three very small kittens. Not newborns, but probably just a week or two old. Two of them were scrambling over one another, playing, and the third was getting a snack from Mom.

"Fred brought his family here," she whispered, soundly deeply satisfied. "I don't think they were born here, but somehow Mama and Papa managed to move their babies here. I'm going to need to buy some cat food tomorrow. Let's leave them alone now. I don't want them to get scared." She backed away from the stall and then quietly left the barn.

He wanted to stay mad at her for leaving the car but couldn't find it in him. "Please don't do that again," he said, when they were outside. "Don't run off."

"I didn't exactly run off," she said.

"Look, I know you don't believe the threats are real, but if they are, it's important that you and I are on the same page. At all times."

"I understand," she said. "I do. You have a job to do and I'm making it more difficult. I'm sorry about that."

Now he really couldn't be mad at her. "Let's get the groceries inside."

It took them two trips. Then, they worked together to get things put away. He took everything that went in the refrigerator while she stocked the cupboards. When they were finished, she turned to him.

"Mavis would be proud of us." She yawned, covering her mouth with her fist. "I think I'll lie down for a while before dinner. I didn't get much sleep last night."

"No problem. I'm going to go sit outside on the patio."

"Veranda," she corrected with a smile. "That's what my mother always calls it."

"The veranda," he repeated, nodding his head. "Okay if I start the steaks around seven?"

"Perfect." She left the kitchen.

He waited until he heard her bedroom door open, then close, before grabbing two potatoes. He scrubbed them up, poked a few holes in them with a fork and stuck them into the oven at 350. Then he grabbed a bottle of water from the fridge and opened the door to go outside.

He owed both his dad and his sister a call. And then he needed to reach out to Brody Donovan, too. They had a bachelor party to plan.

He called his sister first. After their stepmother was arrested, there had been some speculation that Linder Automation would collapse. But the one good thing that Margaret Linder McCann had done was build a fairly strong management team. The corporation would survive intact and people's jobs were saved.

Although not Chandler's. By her choice. She'd found a new job. Same type of work as a computer analyst but better hours, better pay and, best of all, as she was fond of saying, nobody there was selling secrets to the enemy.

The phone rang several times before going to voice mail. He looked at his watch. While it was almost six on the east coast, it was only four in Denver. She was probably hard at work, had her phone on vibrate and didn't even realize she was getting a call. He waited for the beep.

"Hey, Cat Eyes. How's it going? Just checking in. I'll be at this job for another nine days but back in plenty of time to finish the cabin for this shindig you and Ethan seem determined to go through with. Call when you can."

He dialed Ethan next. The man had been one of his

best friends for years, and in six weeks he was going to become his brother-in-law. Ethan, who had landed a job flying medical helicopters, answered on the second ring.

"Hi, Mack," he said.

"Hey, Ethan. You got cold feet yet?"

"Not yet."

It was a stupid question and they both knew it. Ethan wasn't going to get cold feet *ever* about marrying Chandler. It would have been embarrassing how smitten the fool was if it weren't over his sister, who deserved every good thing she got.

"How's the protection detail?" Ethan asked.

Mack started to give him some flip answer but realized that it might be good to have another perspective, especially from someone as solid as Ethan Moore. "Surprising," he admitted.

Ethan paused. "You're never surprised. You're the consummate anticipator, you overprepare for everything."

"It's not a character flaw," Mack protested.

"I know that. What's so surprising?"

"Hope Minnow. I expected… I don't know, I guess I expected a light beer, uncomplicated and not very interesting. She's more of a delicious amber, flavors carefully melded, unique."

"You're comparing her to a microbrew?"

"Only in the broadest sense," Mack said. He couldn't tell Ethan how he really felt. That he'd known Hope Minnow for less than forty-eight hours and he was afraid that he liked her better than any woman that he'd known in his previous thirty-eight years.

Ethan didn't respond. That made Mack nervous.

"Well?" he prompted his friend.

"Well, you don't usually *drink* on the job," Ethan said, his tone carefully neutral.

"I didn't say I was drinking," Mack protested weakly. Hell, he wanted a drink of Hope Minnow. Maybe a whole night of indulging.

Something told him that she would be a very nice cocktail and worth a hell of a hangover.

"Have you heard from Brody?" Mack asked, needing to change the subject.

"Yeah. He's coming back to the States next week. He's going to be a guest at the White House. Guess our boy somehow saved a bunch of lives when there were bombs exploding around him."

"Nerves of steel. He always had them. I got a text from him, asking me to call. He's next on my list. I just wanted to make sure you were taking care of my sister."

"No worries. It's easy work."

Mack smiled. "Talk to you soon." He ended the call and left his phone on the table. He walked back inside to check the potatoes and decided to wait to put the steaks on until Hope was awake. They wouldn't take long. He pulled a bag of lettuce out of the refrigerator. It was one of those where the Caesar dressing and the shredded cheese were in the same package. He opened it, dumped the contents into a bowl and spread the salad dressing around. Then he pulled out the loaf of French bread that Hope had tossed in the cart. He cut half the loaf into slices, buttered the pieces and wrapped them in foil. He'd throw the bread on the grill while the steaks were cooking.

He went back outside and picked up his phone. He pushed the button for Brody Donovan.

"Donovan," his friend answered.

"Dr. Donovan, I presume," Mack said. "*The* Dr. Donovan who has been invited to the White House to be honored."

"I know. Pretty good for a kid who almost failed high-school English."

Brody had almost failed because he'd been in love with the teacher. Fresh out of college, Miss Taper had been a mere four years older than the students she was teaching. She'd walked into the room, smiled at the class and Brody had fallen head over heels in lust. Now, some students might excel when put in the position of trying to impress the teacher. Not Brody. He'd been so enamored that he'd failed to turn in over 50 percent of his homework assignments that semester.

That had not been the last time Brody had been in love. It happened again his first year of medical school.

He and Elle dated for years and he'd evidently figured out how to worship a woman and study for finals because he'd graduated at the top of his class. They were to marry the summer before he started his residency.

But there hadn't been any wedding. Brody had almost been left at the altar. Elle had left town nine days before the wedding, and four months later, his mother returned the wedding gifts that had arrived early.

As far as Mack knew, that was the last serious relationship Brody had. And he never talked about what happened. Gave his friends some line about changing priorities and lack of common ground.

At the time, neither Ethan nor Mack had pushed for the truth. They respected that their friend was guarding his secrets. But they worried. And when he enlisted in the air force following completion of his residency, they wondered what he was running from. And each of them in their own way had tried to ask, but Brody shut them both down. Nicely. But definitely.

Some secrets were evidently not meant to be shared.

"So, you saved a few lives. Big deal," Mack teased.

"All in a day's work," Brody said. "But here's the thing. Tomorrow I leave Afghanistan, headed for Germany. I've got to finish out a few things and then I'll be back in the States for the White House event. They invited my parents, which was nice. Unfortunately, they're out of the country. Dad is researching a book set in Russia. So I have two tickets. I thought of you and Ethan, but Ethan is tied up making your sister happy. Are you in?"

Dinner at the White House. Again. The first time had been almost four years ago and it hadn't been some fancy dinner. No. In a little country where they hated Americans, he'd discovered key intelligence, so sensitive that it warranted a meeting with those at the very top of the food chain.

He'd had pizza and beer in the Oval Office.

The joint looked bigger on television.

"I'm doing protective-services work in New Jersey," Mack said. "Hope Minnow."

There was a pause. "Nice work if you can get it," Brody said, his tone appropriately reverent. "We get *People* magazine here, too."

"She's different than you might think," Mack said immediately.

"I would hope not. She seemed pretty near perfect in that picture. Hell, bring her along. She'll take the attention off me and we'll all be happy."

Most people would jump through hoops for an invitation to dinner at the White House. Mack had no idea how Hope would respond. New York Party Girl would be in her element. Paula would think it was *ridiculous,* to use one of Hope's favorite words.

He hated to disappoint Brody but his first responsibility was to Hope. If she insisted on staying in New Jersey, it wasn't going to be possible to provide that protection from a chair in the west wing dining room. "I'll ask her and let you know."

"Good. We'll talk later." Brody hung up.

Mack put his phone down. He wasn't sure how long he sat before the French doors opened. Hope walked out, looking beautiful in a casual pink dress that tied at the neck. Her feet were bare.

"Hey," he said. He stood up and pulled out a chair for her.

She took it. "Thanks for letting me sleep. I feel a hundred percent better."

"No problem. The potatoes are probably done. I'll start the steaks."

"I'm starving," she admitted.

He pushed his chair back. "Would you like some wine?"

She looked startled and he realized that as comfortable as it all seemed, he may have overstepped. He was, after all, hired help.

"Sorry," he said. "Didn't mean to—"

"I'd love some. I didn't realize I was so awkward at this," she said, with a nervous laugh. "This just proves how ridiculous Sasha was last night. I don't have the skill set to graciously accept a drink. In my own home, no less."

He was a little lost. "What did Sasha do that was ridiculous?"

"It's not what she did, it's what she said. She made some offhand remark about me getting married again."

Married again? "Who's the lucky guy?" he asked, working hard to keep his tone light.

She gave him a blank stare. "Huh?"

"The guy you're going to marry. Who is it?"

She threw her head back and laughed. "There's no guy. Trust me, I'm never getting married again."

His stomach suddenly stopped hurting. "You're young," he said. "You'll change your mind."

She shrugged. "I don't think so. Between what I've experienced myself and what I've seen at Gloria's Path, marriage doesn't look all that appealing."

He could certainly understand her perspective. He took two steps toward the house. "I'm hoping you enjoy the steak enough that you'll feel compelled to do the dishes," he said.

"Consider it done," she said. She turned her chair a little so that she could look over the pool. While it was early evening, the temperature was still in the low eighties. She tilted her head back, allowing her face to catch the very last sunshine of the day.

"Are you intending to go back to the hotel tonight?" he asked.

"Not tonight. I usually volunteer three or four nights a week."

"It's probably a good night to stay home. I checked the weather on my phone and we're supposed to get a heck of a storm."

She didn't answer until he came back with the steaks. "I hope you're right. I have loved storms ever since I was a child," she said. "I distinctly remember my ninth birthday party. I had a sleepover and all night there raged a huge summer storm. My little friends cowered under the covers, screaming every time the lightning cracked. That's when we lived in our old house, which was much smaller. I managed to hang outside my upstairs window, my pajamas getting drenched with rain, watching the tree branches whip around. My friends thought I was crazy."

He figured she'd been a real cute kid. "I'll bet that made your parents happy," he said.

"I don't think they knew."

The steaks sizzled when he put them on the hot grill. "Well, promise me there will no hanging out of the windows tonight."

She smiled and shook her head. "Can't ever promise that."

He sat a bottle of red wine on the table. "This wine takes me back a couple years. I was in northeastern Spain, maybe thirty miles from the coast, the last time I had it. The vineyard that produces it was just down the road. In that area, the ground is more rock than soil and the grapevines were these scraggly-looking things. When I first saw them, I doubted they even produced grapes. But they did. I was there long enough that I saw the harvest."

"You've been a lot of places, I guess," she said, watching him open the wine.

"Yeah. Traveling on Uncle Sam's dime. It was fun, but it got old after a while."

"Is that why you retired?"

"I didn't really retire. I couldn't because I didn't have twenty years in. Lots of people thought I was crazy. Why leave now, they asked, when all I had to do was stay four more years, give a full twenty to Uncle Sam and I could retire with full benefits."

"Why didn't you?"

"I guess I was too impatient. My friend Ethan managed to do that. He enlisted right out of high school and got his twenty in. I, however, chose a different route. I went to the naval academy for four years, but those don't count toward a person's military service."

"But you probably don't regret going to the naval academy?"

"Not one bit. Of course, when I was there I missed my friends, Ethan and Brody. But we kept in touch. Still do."

"So, what's next for you once this assignment is over?" she asked.

"I'm starting a job at Matrice Biomedics as their director of security."

"In Colorado?"

"Yeah. Northwest of Denver. I leased a place in the foothills of the Rockies."

"Sounds nice," she said, taking a sip of the wine he poured. "Oh, this is good."

"Who buys the wine in this house?"

"My mother."

He poured some in his own glass and then lifted it in a toast. "To your mother's good taste."

She laughed. "My mother would appreciate that. She underestimates her own talents. According to her, she's just a girl from Texas who believed until the ripe old age of twenty-two that big hair was the answer to most of the world's problems."

"I've been to a lot of places in the world. Trust me on this, I've met many people who believe stranger things." He flipped the steaks. "Miss Texas, right?"

She took another sip of wine. "I know she didn't tell you, and my father, who married her because she was Miss Texas, now doesn't like to mention it. He wouldn't want to cop to the frailty of worshipping personal beauty."

"How do you know that's why he married her?"

"She told me. When people are very sick, when they think they're dying, they like to reflect upon their lives. And the only thing I could do was listen. She wasn't angry about it. Just the opposite. It amused her that theirs was a marriage based on so little substance that had survived the test of time."

"Forty years, right?"

"Yes, that's right." She looked thoughtful. "You know, my father's fame has been rather recent. Things were different in the old days. Perhaps that helped." She stared off into space for several minutes before switching her gaze back. She didn't make eye contact. Instead, she glanced at the grill. "And maybe it's because he, too, makes a mean steak."

"I imagine marriages have stayed together for less," he said, letting her off the hook. Her eyes took on a sad look whenever she talked about her father.

And he didn't really want Hope Minnow to ever be sad.

Chapter Eleven

They ate in silence, both lost in their own thoughts. "This is delicious," she said, finally looking up from her steak. She reached for the sour cream and put her third teaspoon—yes, third—on her potato. She picked up her glass of wine and realized that it was empty.

Mack reached for the bottle and poured. She held up her hand at half. She wasn't a big drinker. "Thank you," she said. "You've set the bar pretty high."

"You haven't even had my chocolate cake yet."

"You made cake?"

He shook his head. "Had to save something back," he said.

She laughed. And then realized that it had been forever since she'd had a nice dinner with a man and laughed. It felt good. She took a few more bites and pushed her plate away. "I'm stuffed. Absolutely feet-up stuffed."

"Feet-up stuffed?" he repeated.

"Something we used to say in college after we'd pig out. You know, so stuffed you can only sit in the recliner you borrowed from your parents' basement with your feet up and your jeans unbuttoned."

"That's an image I didn't need," he said, pushing his own plate away.

The storm was closer, she could feel it. Darkness had

set in. There would be no pretty reds or lavenders in the sunset tonight. The cloud cover was heavy and the overall impression was a palette of swirling grays.

He picked up his wineglass. He'd drunk less than she had. He was still on his first glass. Probably didn't want to be impaired in any way.

Good cook. Nice guy. Dedicated. Understood the importance of sour cream.

"Tell me about college," he said.

"I went to New York University and fell in love with living in the city. Toward the end of my freshman year, I got a job waitressing at a little restaurant in SoHo and I met the most wonderful people. I was a good student, not a great one, and ultimately got a bachelor's in art history and a master's in visual arts administration."

"Bing mentioned that you worked for the Metropolitan Museum of Art."

"I did. I wanted to stay in Manhattan and working at the Met was really a dream job. I got an apartment with another girl, who had worked at the same restaurant. Meridith had gone to culinary school and she was crazy about food. The rent was so expensive but between the two of us, we managed to cover it. Of course, there wasn't a lot left over for anything else."

"Well educated, struggling professions," Mack said.

"Exactly. Meridith's parents probably could have helped. He was some big lawyer and she was a doctor. But Meridith was determined to make it on her own. That was before my father's rise to fame and my parents had already paid for my education. I certainly wasn't going to ask them to pay for anything else. And it really didn't matter that we didn't have a lot of money. We were having fun."

"Lots to do in the city," Mack said.

"We stayed in a lot. Whatever extra money we had, we spent on food. Meridith was a great cook and it's because of her that I now know how to do more than boil water. She taught me how to make a basic red sauce, then a white sauce. How to roast pork and how to sear scallops. How to make peach cobbler. The list goes on and on."

Mack lifted his glass. "Here's to Meridith."

Hope smiled. It felt good to talk about her friend. "Meridith worked at a restaurant so her weekends were booked. But she had Thursday nights off. Almost every week, on Thursday, we would have some kind of dinner party. Friends from college, friends from work. Sometimes the parties were intimate, sometimes they were raucous affairs with too much tequila that caused the neighbors to pound on the door. That's when we started inviting people from the building."

"Good plan."

"Yes." She took another sip of wine. "It was at one of those parties that I met Wills."

"You don't have to talk about him if it makes you uncomfortable," Mack said quickly.

"It's weird. I never talk about him. With anyone." She looked at her dirty plate. "This is the sour cream talking."

"Oh, yes. In the navy, we frequently used dairy when we were trying to get information from the enemy."

She laughed. "Anyway, Wills came to a party with a friend. When he introduced himself, I realized that I had met him years before, actually several times. My mother, his mother and Mavis, too, had all been sorority sisters at Texas A&M. I knew he was living in the city because my mother kept telling me to *call up that nice boy, William Baylor.* I just never got around to doing it, so it was weird that he just showed up at my apartment one night."

"So you started dating?" Mack asked, his tone giving nothing away.

"We did. And we had fun together. We'd been dating for four months when I took him home to meet my parents at Christmas. My father and Wills hit it off, better than I could have imagined. To make a long story short, within a year, Wills had left his banking position and was working with my father in the ministry that was picking up steam. He commuted from the city for a while, but after a year or so, he moved out to Weatherbie."

"But you stayed in the city?"

"I did. I continued to live with Meridith. My job was going really well. I had been promoted a couple times. A couple years went by and my mother kept suggesting that it was *time*."

Mack didn't say anything.

"So, when Wills asked me to marry him on my twenty-ninth birthday, I said yes. We were married fourteen months later and I moved into the house in Weatherbie and commuted into the city to my job.

"The first time he hit me, I'd gotten back late from the city."

"The first time?" Mack said. "It was more than once?" His voice was hard.

"Yes. I'm not very proud of that. Makes me seem like a bit of a doormat, doesn't it?"

He reached out for her hand and it seemed the most natural thing in the world to let him hold it. "*You* were not the problem," he said.

"I know. Anyway, I'd gone to visit Meridith and her new husband. They had carried on the tradition of Thursday night parties. Wills knew I was going. I'd invited him to go with, but he was too busy with the church. My father's occasional appearance on television had turned into a weekly show and the money was flowing in."

His thumb was stroking her palm. It was enough to give her the courage to finish.

"I had a wonderful time, but when I got home I could tell that Wills was in a terrible mood, one of the worst I'd ever seen. He said that a big donor had decided that he wasn't going to fulfill his pledge. This was a donor that Wills had personally courted."

She paused, still able to remember that night like it was yesterday. "I wanted to give him something else to think about so I started showing him the pictures that I'd taken on my cell phone of Meridith's new apartment. She and her husband had done a good job decorating it. I had forgotten that Meridith had used my phone to take a couple pictures of me dancing with her brother-in-law. He'd been showing me his steps. He was taking dance lessons to surprise his wife."

"Baylor didn't like the pictures?" Mack asked.

"I tried to explain that it was Meridith's brother-in-law, who was happily married with two children. He refused to listen and we argued. Still, I was unprepared when he backhanded me across the face."

Mack's grip tightened but his face showed no emotion.

"It happened so fast and after it was over, he was so apologetic. And like a fool, I let it go. He said he loved me, he was practically sobbing. He begged me to forgive him. And I did. At least I told him I did. I'm not sure if you ever really forgive someone for doing that. It stays in the back of your mind, nagging at you, coming back at you when you least expect it."

"And you didn't tell anybody?" Mack asked.

"No. Not my mother, my father, or even Meridith. I was embarrassed and, as crazy as it now seems, even thought that somehow I'd played a role. I shouldn't have gone to the city. I shouldn't have danced with Meridith's brother-in-law. Anyway, we never talked about it again."

She sat silently for a couple minutes, staring at their linked hands. Mack's hand was bigger and his skin was darker. The bruise on his index finger was healing.

"It was just a few months later that my mom got sick. For a while, I tried to balance everything. I worked during the day and when I got back to Weatherbie, I went to my mom's house. I was there every weekend. It took a toll on me, plus my mom was continuing to fail. Four months into the cancer diagnosis, I quit my job so that I could tend to Mom full-time."

She looked up. "Wills said he supported that decision. But we'd gotten used to living on two incomes. I could have asked my parents for money because by that time their own financial situation had greatly improved, but I didn't want to do that. Wills and I started to argue about money but he never hit me."

"Until he did again," Mack said softly.

"Yes. Wills was now regularly appearing on my father's television show. He had asked me to pick up some dry cleaning, but I had taken my mother to a chemotherapy appointment and we got caught in traffic coming out of the city. The dry cleaner was closed by the time I pulled into the lot. I didn't give it much thought, knowing that he had another dozen shirts in his closet. My mom was so sick by then that it was hard to worry about anything else. That night I spent most of the night at my mom's and had gotten home around two in the morning. A couple hours later, I was in bed, trying to catch a little sleep, when Wills discovered that his favorite blue shirt wasn't there."

She pulled her hand back. He let it go. She couldn't

touch Mack, not now. "He'd dragged me out of bed by my hair and just went crazy. I fought back but he was bigger and he...he got the best of me."

"Hope," Mack said, his voice sounding hoarse. "You don't—"

"After he left me lying on the bedroom floor, I managed to pull myself up and I called my dad. I knew I needed a doctor. He came to the house and I told him what had happened. He took me to the emergency room, not in Weatherbie, but in Hazelton, two suburbs away. I was in so much pain and in shock, I wasn't really tracking what he was doing. He said it would be better to get treatment there. He didn't come in with me, just dropped me off at the door. It didn't dawn on me until the next day that it was *better* because we were someplace where people weren't as likely to connect that Hope Baylor was Reverend Archibald Minnow's daughter."

"I'm sorry," Mack said.

"Well, you pretty much know the rest. At his request, I told the nurses that I'd fallen down the basement stairs and I ignored the knowing looks in their eyes. One of them gave me information on Gloria's Path. After I got out of the hospital, my father arranged for me to go to a hotel to recover."

"That's when you went to Gloria's Path?"

"Yes. I didn't cancel my hotel room, though. I let my father pay for it. That's when my rather obsessive habit of spending my father's money began."

"Didn't your mother wonder where you were?"

"My father told her that I was out of town, doing a one-time consulting assignment for my old employer."

"What about Baylor?"

"He tried to call me, sometimes I'd get twenty-five calls a day from him. But I wouldn't see him. I started divorce proceedings immediately and communicated with him only through my attorney. I never went back to the house. I simply bought new clothes and moved into my old bedroom. I told my mother and Mavis that Wills and I had grown apart. My mom was certainly sad, but given that she was in a fight for her life, she had other things to worry about. Most everyone thought it was a very amicable split because Wills continued to work in the ministry, as my father's assistant."

"I was pretty damned civilized about the whole thing. It's really a good skill to be able to remain outwardly calm even when you're inwardly furious."

"I don't know what your father was thinking," Mack said. "If I'd seen that, I'd have killed Baylor."

Chapter Twelve

Mack said it with such solid conviction that she believed him. He would not let someone hurt his family. Her father had evidently felt differently. But what did it matter? Old water, old bridge.

She pushed back her chair and gathered both their plates. He started to push his chair back.

"I've got these," she said quickly. "A deal is a deal." She needed to get away from Mack and get a little perspective. Blame it on the sour cream or the wine or the fact that she'd simply just needed to finally tell someone. Whatever the reason, she'd shared a lot and was emotionally spent. "I said I'd do the dishes," she added, knowing that she sounded a little harsh.

"Okay," he said, settling back into his chair.

Hope half expected Mack to follow her inside. But he remained at the table, staring off into the distance. She turned on the water, let it get hot, then rinsed the plates and silverware. Then she loaded everything into the stainless-steel dishwasher, carefully placing the heavy stoneware in the racks.

She was tired. That explained it. The brief nap she'd had this afternoon had helped, but she was still several hours shy of the six hours of sleep a day that it took to keep her body going.

She folded the dish towel, hung it over the bar on the stove and looked through the French doors that led to the veranda. Mack was still sitting at the table. His cell phone to his ear. He'd turned his chair so that he was able to see her working in the kitchen.

Maybe he was talking to her father. She suspected that they'd prearranged times to talk. Was her father getting an all-is-well-in-Weatherbie report? Somehow, she doubted that Mack was offering the details. *Had a nice steak dinner with your daughter. We drank some wine. Had a few laughs. She told me what an ass you are.*

Too much information, for sure.

Was he waiting for her to join him again? Deliberately, she turned away. It had been a nice dinner, but there was no need to give him any reason to think that she wanted to extend the evening. She had things to do, her own calls to make.

She shut off the lights in the kitchen and walked upstairs to her room. She sat on the edge of her bed and reached for her cell on the nightstand table. She'd tried Mavis earlier to see how things were going at her sister's house, but hadn't been able to reach the woman. She hadn't left a message. She scrolled through her numbers and hit Call.

It rang four times before going to voice mail again. Instead of hanging up, she waited for the beep. "Hi, Mavis," Hope said. "Just checking in to make sure you got there okay. Hope your sister's husband is doing better. Call if you need anything."

She knew that Mavis was probably working like crazy to take care of things. Probably baking and cleaning and finding time in the middle of all that to visit her brother-in-law and pamper her sister a bit. The woman was a dynamo. She defined the words *active senior*. It was such a shame that she'd lost her husband and was alone during what was supposed to be her golden years. And she didn't seem inclined to go down that path again.

Hope distinctly remembered walking in on her mother and Mavis during one of their afternoon teas. They'd been talking about the neighbor woman across the road who was in her late sixties and recently remarried. Her mom had gently suggested to Mavis that perhaps it was time to start dating again.

Mavis, who had been standing at the sink, steeping the bags of tea, had gotten the oddest expression on her face. Then she'd seen Hope and her expression cleared.

Hope could understand the feeling. She hadn't been kidding when she'd told Mack that she was done with marriage.

She put her cell down, confident that Mavis would return the call when she was able to. She got up, walked across the room and opened the door that led to her balcony. Of all the space in the house, she loved this the most. It was just big enough for two lounge chairs and a few plants that she'd potted herself. Because it faced the west, she got the benefit of the most amazing sunsets.

The storm was getting closer. The air felt hot and wild and she could smell the approaching rain. Tonight, she'd stay out as long as she possibly could, hopefully for the duration of the storm. She didn't mind getting wet.

She closed her eyes, wanting to use her other senses to experience the storm. She deliberately slowed her breathing, drawing air deep into her lungs. Holding it for just a second. Letting go.

It was dark when she woke up to a sharp crack of lightning and then a subsequent explosion. The lights in her bedroom went out. Same for the tall yard light.

As she was thinking that the lightning had likely hit a

nearby transformer, knocking out their power and likely their neighbors', too, incessant pounding started at her bedroom door.

"Hope?" Mack yelled. There was a short break in the pounding. "Open the door or I'm shooting the lock off."

"Hang on," she yelled. She hurried across her pitch-black bedroom. She felt for the doorknob, unlocked it and swung the door open.

Mack shined a flashlight in her eyes.

She put up her hand.

"Sorry," he said, lowering the light and pointing it at the floor. "Are you okay?"

"I'm fine." There was just enough illumination reflecting upward to see that he looked rumpled and sexy. His T-shirt was pulled out of his jeans, as if the storm may have woken him up from a deep sleep.

Tempting.

"Thanks for checking," she added, before she tried to shut the door.

He stuck his foot out, stopping the door's momentum. "I want you to come downstairs."

"Why?"

"Without power, the security system won't work. You should have a battery backup but you don't. I want you downstairs where I can see you."

"What time is it?" she said, attempting to get her bearings.

"Eleven," he said.

She could hear thunder rumbling and then another crack of lightning. The storm was very close and she didn't intend to miss it.

"I'm fine," she said. She tried to close the door again but it was like trying to push against a brick wall. "Good grief," she said. She turned around, saw the flicker of light and knew that he was tracking her movements with his flashlight. She walked back to her balcony.

She took a seat on one of the lounge chairs. Within seconds, he was lowering himself down on the other one. "I guess it's slightly safer than hanging out the window," he muttered.

The first splatter of rain hit her bare lower legs. She waited for him to add that she was going to get soaked. But he didn't say anything.

The wind was whipping through the trees and when the rain came, it hit at a slant, a driving shower. It was a cacophony of sensation: the rumble of the thunder, the crack of the lightning, the whistle of wind, coupled with the shock of the cold rain on her warm skin.

She felt more alive than she had in years. More carefree. Maybe even reckless.

The hard rain lasted for maybe ten minutes and stopped almost as quickly as it had started. By this time, she was soaked and knew he had to be, as well. But still, he'd said nothing.

Suddenly, she heard him shift on his chair, get up and walk into her bedroom. He returned with some soft towels from her bathroom and the blanket from the end of her bed. "You're going to get cold," he said, handing it all to her.

She reached up. Their hands connected.

And a flash, every bit as intense as the lightning they'd witnessed, shot up her arm. Instinctively, she pushed her fingers between his, wrapping them over the edge of his hand.

Then she pulled her arm back, pulling his hand and arm, his body, toward her. She heard his breath catch but he didn't resist.

She rested their linked hands on her heart, which was

thumping in her chest. To keep his balance, he'd put one knee on the lounge chair. She could feel it next to her bare leg. She sensed, more than saw, that his face was less than a foot from hers. She could feel the tension in his hand and knew that maybe she'd managed to shake cool, calm Mack McCann just a little.

"Hope?" he asked.

"Shush," she said gently. Then she leaned forward and, with her free hand, cupped his chin. His face was wet, slick with rain. With the pad of her thumb, she felt for his lips. It was so dark, so erotic to be touching him, learning him.

"Kiss me," she whispered.

When he hesitated, she used her hand to pull his face closer. And when his lips brushed against hers, nerve endings that had been dormant for a long time starting singing. She could feel her body heat up and moisture begin to gather between her legs.

His lips hovered and she felt his warm, sweet breath on her face. He was about to pull back, she could feel it.

Hope Minnow, who had been living in limbo for the last two years, took control. She moved his hand, which she still had clenched tight in hers, to her breast. She arched her back, pressing her aching body into his warm grasp.

"Sweet mother of God," he said, running his thumb across the wet material that was molded to her skin. Her nipple, already hard, responded to his touch.

Then he kissed her. Hard. And her body came alive.

And still, he was holding back. She could feel it. "I need you to know something," she said, her mouth close to his ear. "I haven't had sex in two years. And if you turn me down, it's going to be devastating to my self-esteem. Worse even than Hopeless Fish Bait."

He was still for several seconds. Then he felt for her hand, took it in his and moved it down his body. He arched his hips toward her and pressed her hand against him. He was so hard. It was erotic and bold and sensation swamped her needy body. "You do this to me," he said, his voice low, sexy. "You. How's that working for your self-esteem, Hopeless?"

"Pretty good," she said, and she nipped at his lower lip.

He took charge, pulling at the tie of her sundress, peeling the wet material down her body until she was bare to the waist. The warm night air washed over her.

They didn't need light. He used his hands and his mouth to learn her body. Soft licks to the inner skin of her elbows. A brush of lips across her collarbone, a nip on her earlobe. Long succulent feasts on her nipples. Deep kisses with his tongue in her mouth.

And when her body was literally writhing with want, he gathered her up and carried her inside to the bed, leaving the door to the balcony open. He laid her down and she could hear him removing his clothes. Then he pulled her dress off all the way, her panties.

And then his mouth did all kinds of delicious things to her lower half until finally he stopped. She heard the rip of a condom and then finally, finally, he was inside of her.

He moved gently, letting her adjust, letting her get used to him. And when he was finally seated deep, he put his hands under her rear, pulled her apart even more and started to move.

When she came, it was shockingly intense, so much so that she thought she might have actually blacked out for a moment. He let her ride out the moment.

"Okay?" he asked, his voice husky with need.

"Oh, yes," she said. "That was better than sour cream." She could feel his smile against her shoulder. Then he began to move again and she could feel him inside of her, even bigger, more powerful. She felt full and stretched and when she arched and took him even deeper, she could feel the shudder roll down the powerful muscles of his back.

She kissed his shoulder and realized that the rain had dried but now his body was slick with sweat.

"I'm going to come," he groaned.

He moved inside of her, even faster now, his strokes long. She felt her own need build again and she clenched him tight. As she exploded around him, he stiffened, his body no longer able to resist.

MACK DRIFTED BACK to consciousness with the realization that he'd just had the most amazing sex of his life. With Hope Minnow. His head would have likely spun if he had the strength to lift it.

He had a thousand questions. Should he apologize? Plead temporary insanity? Admit that his knees were still weak? Wait fifteen minutes and go for round two?

The biggest question of all: Why had Hope waited two years to have sex, only to have sex with him?

A better man would have said no. He'd intended to until she'd pushed her lovely breast into his hand and literally begged him.

She hadn't been drunk or impaired in any way. He had absolutely nothing to feel guilty about.

With the exception that he was supposed to be guarding her.

They were going to have to talk about it, but maybe not right now. He pulled away from Hope and went to the bathroom to clean up the best he could without the use of water. They would have to wait for the electricity to come back on before the well would work.

It didn't take him but a second to realize that he had a problem. *They* potentially had a problem. He stood in the dark and felt his heart rate accelerate.

The condom broke.

Chapter Thirteen

What the hell was he going to tell her? Could he hide something like this? Absolutely not.

On his way back to bed, he closed the balcony door and locked it. No sense giving her an opportunity to make a leap for it. Then he climbed back into bed.

Hope had turned on her side. He moved close, spooning her, his arm around her waist as he pulled her close.

"Hope?" he asked.

"Yes," she said, sounding sleepy.

Not for long. He was about to drop a bomb. "I think we may have an issue."

She turned in his arms and faced him. "What?" she whispered, as if she thought someone had managed to sneak in the house.

No, *that* would be easy to deal with. There was no good way to say it. "The condom broke."

"What?" she said again, only this time it had a totally different ring.

"Are you on any type of birth control?" he asked.

"No. Of course not. I haven't been having sex," she said indignantly. She sat up in bed.

He scrambled to sit up, as well. He wanted to reach out and hold her, but didn't know if his touch would be welcome.

He heard a humorless chuckle. "Well, I guess there's an upside. Everything I've done up to this point to irritate my dad will be child's play if I'm suddenly an unwed mother."

His child would have a father. A father and a mother that were married. "It wouldn't have to be that way," he said tentatively. When she didn't answer, he decided to go for broke. "If there's a child, there's a reason to get married."

"Oh, good grief. I'm not getting married again, Mack. I told you that."

If she were pregnant, all bets were off. "We may be worrying about nothing," he said.

He could feel the air leave her body. "You're probably right. I wasn't on birth control when I was married and I never got pregnant. It's probably fine."

She lay back down, but not close enough that he could hold her. She was crowding her edge of the bed. The message was loud and clear. Cuddling time was over. He lay back as well, careful not to cross over the invisible middle line in the bed.

A child. Tonight he may have fathered a child.

That changed everything.

THE LIGHTS CAME back on at 3:07 a.m. Hope had rolled over to her stomach, with one arm flung out. She was still blissfully naked and he took a moment to study her.

Her skin was tan against the white sheets and so soft. He could see the ridge of her spine and then the gentle curve of her butt. Her long hair spilled over her shoulders, almost covering her face.

Gorgeous.

So damn sexy. And like a crazy fool, he imagined her

body, ripe with child. Her breasts heavy, her belly growing with new life.

His child.

He eased himself out of bed, careful not to wake her. He pulled on his jeans but didn't bother zipping them. He walked downstairs and shut off the lights that had been on before the blackout. He reset the security system.

He went back upstairs and saw that Hope was awake, sitting up in bed. The sheet was pulled up to her neck and her face was very pale.

"Morning," he said, working hard for casual. His insides were churning.

"Good morning. I didn't dream our conversation, did I?"

"No."

"Oh, good Lord." She put a hand over her eyes. "I cannot believe that the first time I have sex in years, the condom breaks. Who has that kind of luck? You know who? Hopeless Fish Bait, that's who."

"I guess," he said, trying to keep it light. But then he realized that there was something that he really needed to say, he really needed her to understand. "Listen, Hope. I want you to know that if you are pregnant, you don't have to do this alone. I'll be there."

She stared at him. "We can never do this again."

"Let's not be rash," he said.

She shook her head. "Listen, I realize that this is my fault. I asked you to have sex with me. I'm a big girl, Mack. I take responsibility for my own actions. I've potentially put both of us in a very difficult situation."

"Don't beat yourself up. Nobody put a gun to my head. If anybody needs to feel bad about what happened, it's me. I'm supposed to be ensuring that you stay safe. But the reality is, that while there's probably plenty of blame to go around, we are both single adults. Single adults can have sex. We shouldn't feel badly about it. In fact, I think we should be kind of happy. This was really great sex."

She smiled. Finally.

It was going to be okay. He took a step toward the bed when the phone on his belt vibrated. Who the hell was calling him at three-thirty in the morning? He looked at the number. Brody. He read the text.

Are you and the lovely Hope M. coming to the dinner? I have to notify the WH. They need time to run security checks on her. You evidently still pass.

He supposed now was as good a time as any to ask. "May I?" he said, motioning to the edge of the bed. He waited until she nodded.

He sat. "My good friend Dr. Brody Donovan has been patching up soldiers on the front lines for more than ten years. He's recently left the air force but he's going to be honored at the White House next week at a dinner. I was wondering…well, I was wondering if you'd like to attend. With me."

"Dinner at the White House?" she repeated.

"Yes. Dinner. A few speeches. Obligatory clapping. Good desserts as I recall."

She let go of her sheet and it slipped several inches, but not far enough that he had a really good glimpse of her beautiful breasts. "You recall?" she repeated. "You've been to the White House before."

He waved a hand. "It was years ago. Something informal. But I do remember the cheesecake."

"I'm busy," she said.

"I didn't even tell you which night," he said, attempting to keep his tone even.

"It doesn't matter. I'll be busy."

He tapped his index finger on the white sheets. "Why?" he asked finally.

She sighed. "Is it important? Listen, you're here for another week or so. I don't really think that my lack of attendance at this event is going to impact the future course of your life."

"I just thought you might enjoy it. And I thought," he said, his throat feeling tight, "that maybe *this* made a difference."

She shook her head. "You said it yourself. Single adults have sex. This wasn't special, Mack."

"Wasn't special," he repeated. Then wanted to kick himself for rising to the bait.

"No," she said. "Listen, I would like to get some more sleep. Can you make sure you shut the door tight when you leave?" She turned over in bed, giving him her back.

He knew he could easily force her to give him her undivided attention. But that wasn't something Mack would ever do.

Regardless of how much her rejection hurt.

He left the room without another word, closing the door quietly behind him.

HOPE WAITED A full minute after hearing the door shut before she flipped over in bed. In the darkness, she stared upward. *Dinner at the White House.* Her father would be ecstatic. It would be the kind of publicity that he regularly tried to buy.

What the hell was Mack thinking?

Never mind that. What had she been thinking? She'd slept with a man who lived in a world where he regularly received invitations to the White House. People who lived in that kind of world were ripe for public scrutiny. More of what she'd been living since her father's rise to fame.

She couldn't do it. Not anymore.

But she hadn't needed to be so damn petty about it. Hadn't needed to dismiss the best sex she'd ever had. Hadn't needed to make Mack feel badly when she, quite frankly, ladies and gentlemen of the jury, had been the aggressor.

She started to swing her legs over the side of the bed and stopped. What the hell was she going to do if she were pregnant with Mack's child?

It wasn't as if she didn't want a child. It wasn't something she generally talked about, but at thirty-four she could feel her biological clock starting to wind down. Just last week she read an article about a television star who was having her first baby at thirty-six. It said that everyone over the age of thirty-five was now considered high-risk.

Time was running out. But still, she'd never considered getting pregnant. Children needed two parents. She'd simply been spouting off when she'd let Mack think that she was cool with raising a child on her own.

She lay back down and stared upward. It reminded her of when she'd been a little girl. Her father would walk her to her room, read her a story and, right before he left, she would lie in her bed and stare at the ceiling. He would stand at the door and listen to her prayers.

She folded her hands. "Dear God…" she began.

Chapter Fourteen

Mack took his aggression out on his arm and leg muscles, using the treadmill and the weight machine as his weapons of choice. He worked his body until fatigue would have made additional exercise dangerous.

Then he dragged his body off for a cold shower.

It appeared he was going to be taking a lot of them. *We can never do this again.*

It would have been easy to pack his things and go lick his wounds in private. But there was no way. The stakes had always been high. Now they were even higher. Hope could be pregnant with his child.

What the hell would her parents say? And Bing? Would he regret asking Mack to come in the first place?

None of that could be helped. They would sort through all of it.

Chandler would be thrilled to be an aunt. His dad would be happy for him. Brody and Ethan would have cigars ready.

Assuming he could convince Hope to marry him. Because he wasn't interested in being a long-distance dad, somebody his child associated with the airport.

After his shower, he got dressed and cooked some breakfast. There was no sign of Hope and he figured she was avoiding him. If she intended to go into town to help Serena move into her new apartment, she was going to have to get over that fast. The rules hadn't changed. Where she went, he went.

He'd just have to be a little more careful *how far* he followed.

At twelve-thirty, Hope walked into the kitchen. Mack looked up from the newspaper that he wasn't really reading. She carried Paula's clothes and wig in her hands. She again wore her black leggings, but this time she had on a long gray-and-black silky T-shirt. Her hair was piled on top of her head.

"Morning," he said.

"Good morning," she answered. She pulled a glass from the cupboard and filled it with water from the faucet. She drained the glass in two long drinks.

He knew he was in for a bad time of it when even the working of her soft, sexy throat made him hard.

"Would you like some lunch?" he asked. He needed to do something besides stare at her.

"Just some toast," she said. "I'll get it."

He didn't respond. Just looked at his hands. He listened while she pulled the bread out of its wrapper and pushed the toaster lever down. Heard the pop. Then, the turn of the lid to the peanut butter.

She surprised him when she pulled out the chair next to him. "I'm sorry," she said.

He waited.

"I didn't mean to hurt you."

"I'm a big boy, Hope. I'll survive it," he said, his tone harsher than he intended. He took a breath, channeling the control that was usually easy for him. It felt out of reach.

"I know you will. But I could have been much kinder."

He took a chance. "It's not kindness that I'm looking

for from you. I just want you to have an open mind about the possibilities."

"This got complicated quickly," she said. "I want you to know that last night was wonderful and…"

He waited.

"And it was also a mistake. Those terms are not necessarily mutually exclusive."

He could feel his damn throat struggle to work. "Sometimes things aren't as complicated as we make them."

She smiled but it didn't reach her pretty eyes. "Listen, we need to get going. I assume that you're coming with me to move Serena into her new apartment. I have a request."

"Okay," he said. As long as it didn't involve anything that would compromise her safety, he was willing to listen.

"I don't want to have any more discussion about a possible pregnancy. We'll know soon enough. I'd like to just pretend that it's not even a possibility. And, of course, neither one of us should talk to anybody else about it."

He didn't need to talk about it, but it was in the forefront of his mind. He couldn't help that. "That's fine. Consider it done." He looked at her toast. "You going to eat that?"

She pushed it toward the middle of the table. "I'm not really hungry." She pulled her cell phone out of her purse. She looked at the screen and frowned.

"What's wrong?" he asked.

"I left a message for Mavis and she hasn't called me back yet. I'm worried about her."

"Mavis seems as if she can take care of herself pretty well."

She put her phone away. "You're right. I'm sure she'll call soon."

They left the house and drove into town. They didn't talk until they reached the hotel. Mack drove around it twice before he parked in a spot a block away from the front door.

Serena was waiting for them in the lobby. The two women exchanged hugs.

"I didn't realize you'd still be here," Serena said to him. "Must be wonderful to have such a nice long visit with your sister."

"Wonderful," Mack echoed, not making eye contact with Hope. He picked up Serena's suitcase. Serena carried a box. It was the kind that had cutouts in the sides, making it easier to carry. It also gave him a look into the box. It was filled with books, a crystal vase and a couple of picture frames turned inward so he couldn't see the photos.

He'd always traveled light. The military taught a person how to do that. But he'd always had the security of knowing that his stuff was back home in storage. If he ultimately could only have one box, what would he take? Pictures of his family? A given. Proof that his grades at the academy had earned him a spot on the superintendent's list most semesters? Not likely. His old Jimmy Buffett CDs, almost antiques by now? For sure.

He used his key fob to pop open the trunk. They stowed her things inside and then got into the car. Hope gave him directions.

"Wayne sent me a text, wanting to know if I'd rented an apartment," Serena said. "I told him I did."

"Did you tell him where?" Hope asked.

"No. He didn't ask, either. He said he'd registered for some internet dating site. I asked him which one but he wouldn't say."

It was like high school, Mack thought. Boy acts bad.

Girl gets mad and kicks Boy to curb. Boy doesn't want to idle at curb and schemes to get Girl back. Boy acts disinterested and says he's moving on, hoping Girl comes crawling back.

Except the stakes were a lot higher than not having a date for the homecoming dance. When Wayne acted up, he started using Serena as a punching bag. If Serena went back, it was anyone's guess how bad her injuries might be the next time.

He could tell Hope was tracking along the same lines. "Does it matter what site?" she asked gently.

In his rearview mirror, Mack could see Serena shrug. "I guess not," she said.

Mack drove to the apartment. He maneuvered through the lot, passing several empty parking spaces. Nothing seemed unusual. It was about half-full. Nobody was loitering near the doors. He knew he hadn't been followed from the hotel.

Safe enough. He parked in an empty spot, twenty feet away from the nearest car.

"My brother likes to find the perfect parking spot," Hope said, evidently trying to explain his behavior.

He didn't think Serena cared. She was staring out the window, looking at her new eight-unit apartment building, likely remembering the house that she'd run from. Comparing. Maybe coming up short.

He waited for her to say that she couldn't do it. Instead, she opened her purse and he could see her clench a stack of twenties.

Hope opened her purse, too. She pulled out ten one-hundred-dollar bills. He knew she hadn't gone to the bank. She must keep a stash somewhere in her room, for occasions just like this. She handed the money to Serena.

The woman's hand shook when she reached for the

money. "I don't know when I'll be able to repay it," she said softly.

"It doesn't matter," said Hope. "I know you will."

They got out. Like before, the landlord was waiting for them inside. The transaction went pretty fast. Serena turned over the money, the landlord gave her the key and a potted geranium for her small balcony. Then he left.

Standing in her kitchen, Serena turned in circles. "Home sweet home," she said, her voice sounding small in the empty space. Forlorn. "I guess I'll have to figure something out for furniture."

"Gloria's Path works with a secondhand store. I'll arrange for them to drop off a couch, a bed and a dresser, as well as some dishes, pots and pans, bedding and towels. That will get you started."

"Thank you." Serena's eyes had tears in them. "I wish I would have thought about a coffeepot. I love coffee," she added, her tone wistful.

"You know what," Hope said, "Mack and I need to pick up a few things. We'll grab a coffeepot and some coffee from Tate Drugs and drop them off here on our way back."

He could see that Serena was close to her breaking point and perhaps Hope sensed it, too, because they made a fast exit. Once they were back in the car, they sat in silence.

"It's weird," he said finally. "She's so immature at times and yet, so mature at other times."

"Yes. She's only 26. I guess that's normal."

"Where's Tate Drugs?" he asked.

She gave him directions as he drove. She took off her wig and she shimmied out of her shirt and pants. It made him remember how he'd undressed her the night before, how terribly erotic it had been to untie her dress, to feel the wet, heavy material fall to her waist, knowing that her breasts were fully exposed to the night air, and to him.

"How come Paula never goes shopping?" he asked, reaching for the mundane.

"I don't know. Hope shops. Paula helps battered women." She took off the ugly tennis shoes and put on sandals.

He gave her a sidelong look. "You know that Hope and Paula are the same woman?"

She looked down her pretty nose at him. "Thank you, Dr. Phil."

He drove into the parking lot of the mom-and-pop drugstore, the kind that only existed anymore in small towns that hadn't caught the attention of Target and Walmart. It was part of a strip mall with four other retailers.

They got out of the car and walked across the parking lot that was in need of some repair. The woman at the front counter looked up when they opened the door. He caught the flare of recognition in her eyes.

"Hi, Hope," she said.

"Hey, Jane," Hope responded politely, not stopping.

"Friend?" he asked quietly once they were past.

"Acquaintance. We went to high school together. Four years of gym proved that she was a better soccer player than me but couldn't play tennis to save her life."

"How's her golf?"

"Don't ask."

It was a good day for golf but not a good day for shopping. The store was warm, almost stuffy. The high for the day was expected to be eighty-five and it had to be close to that already.

They found the aisle for coffeepots. There were only

three brands to choose from. Hope dutifully read the descriptions on each box before finally picking the basic, least expensive model.

"You're ruining your image," he whispered.

"I know. But Paula is really buying this. And Paula is a good bargain shopper."

"I don't know how you keep all this straight in your head."

It took them several minutes to find the coffee. It was at the end of an aisle, along with a few boxes of cereal, some macaroni and cheese that went in the microwave and small round tins of mixed nuts.

Mack looked at the price of the coffee and saw that it was twice what they would pay for it at a grocery store. He didn't suggest doing any comparison shopping. He sure as hell didn't want to take the chance of running into Hope's ex-husband again.

Yesterday, he'd managed to hold back. Now, after holding her body, knowing first-hand how delicately she was made, it made him crazy to think that she'd been beaten by the man. He desperately wanted to smash his fist in Baylor's mouth.

Hope picked up some toothpaste and a few other items. They rounded an aisle and ran smack-dab into the home-pregnancy testing kits. Remembering his promise, he didn't say a word. He saw Hope look at them for several long seconds. Then she turned to him. "First of all, I'm not pregnant," she whispered. "Secondly, I sure as hell can't buy one of these here. The whole town will know in minutes." Then she hurried out of the aisle.

They were almost out of the store when she remembered that she needed cat food. The store only carried small bags of dry food. "Better than nothing," Hope said.

"Fred's probably doing his best to catch mice. This will be the backup plan."

Jane checked them out. "How have you been?" she asked.

"Great. You?" Hope replied.

"Good. Just working, you know." She rang the cat food through. "Must have a cat."

"I do," Hope said, sounding happy. When Jane gave her the total, she pulled out the correct change. Jane bagged their items, giving him several looks in the process.

He didn't say anything. He wasn't sure what *B* word Hope would use today to describe him. Brief encounter. Bad mistake. He didn't like any of those.

Baby daddy.

He was losing it.

"Thanks, Jane," Hope said, picking up her sack. "See you around." She pushed open the glass door.

Mack glanced over the parking lot. He didn't see anything unusual.

They were thirty feet from the store when Hope bent down suddenly, to shake a rock out of her sandal. At that exact moment, a bullet hit the store window behind them, shattering the glass.

Chapter Fifteen

"Get down!" he yelled. He leaped toward Hope, twisting his body so that when his momentum carried both of them to the pavement, he took the hardest hit. He felt the hot pavement grind into his back and knew he was going to have a knot on the back of his head.

Once on the ground, he quickly got to his feet. Bent at the waist, he pulled Hope up and hauled her in between a blue Toyota Camry and a pale gray Mazda.

A woman two rows over started screaming and someone hit the hazard button on their car keys, starting a loud beeping.

He looked at Hope. Her face was white and her eyes were big. "Are you okay?" he asked. Without thought, he looked at her absolutely flat stomach. She had her hand splayed across her abdomen.

"I'm okay," she said. "I am," she reassured him.

He pulled his gun from its holster. "Stay down," he instructed. He raised up, looked in the direction from where the shot had come. A gray van and a blue SUV were the only vehicles moving in the parking lot. They were going in opposite directions.

He wanted to get closer, to force a confrontation with the gunman, but he didn't move. It was possible that the shot had been a distraction, something to separate him from her. If he pursued the shooter, a second assailant might make his move on Hope. Mack wouldn't take that chance.

He saw a man who might be a manager run out of the store, a cell phone to his ear. Mack pulled his own cell phone off his belt. He scanned his numbers, found the one he was looking for. He had Police Chief Anderson on the line within seconds.

Mack swiftly identified who he was, why he was calling and their location. He also described the two vehicles that had been in the lot. He got an assurance that the chief would be there quickly.

By the time he finished the call, the first cop car arrived, sirens blaring, lights going. An ambulance followed them.

Even then, he kept Hope down, protected by the cars. It would take the chief a few minutes to get there and he didn't intend to talk to anybody else.

However, he wasn't counting on the woman who'd been screaming suddenly pointing at them and yelling, "They were shooting at them."

That got everybody's attention. He put his gun away.

He helped Hope stand up. That's when he got his first good look at her and realized that the right knee on her leggings was shredded. And he could see blood.

"Damn it, you're hurt," he said. He could see a male and a female officer approaching. He made sure his shirt was covering his gun. He didn't want them to start panicking if they saw that he was carrying.

"It's a scratch," she responded, waving her hand.

"Sir, ma'am, we'd like to ask you some questions," the male officer said.

Mack shook his head. "Not until somebody looks at her knee," he said.

The two cops looked at each other. Likely they weren't used to somebody telling them no. Finally, the woman nodded. "Okay." She waved a paramedic over. It was a girl of about eighteen and Mack almost demanded that they send someone more experienced, more knowledgeable.

But he kept his mouth shut because the young woman seemed very competent. She checked Hope's pulse, her blood pressure and her pupils. Evidently satisfied that there was no immediate need for concern, she carefully cut away the material, cleaned out the cuts and placed a bandage on Hope's knee.

Mack stood two feet away, watching everything.

"You're going to want to put some ice on that," the paramedic said. "I usually have some cold bags but somebody must have forgotten to restock them. When you get home, twenty minutes on, twenty minutes off. Sooner the better."

"I will. Thank you so much," Hope said, being her naturally kind self.

Mack wasn't feeling kind. He wanted blood. But he forced himself to remain calm, to not generate any more attention than they already had.

After the paramedic finished, the male and female officers approached a second time. When asked, both he and Hope provided their names and showed their driver's licenses as identification. He could tell the minute the officers connected that the victim was the daughter of Weatherbie's most known celebrity.

The male officer became more differential, perceptibly more polite. The female officer just the opposite. He could see the disdain in her eyes that she wasn't trying very hard to hide.

He knew that Hope picked up on it right away. She

remained polite but the natural warmth that he'd come to expect was missing. She was distant and he could see how others would perceive that she thought she was better than everybody else.

They were saved from having to answer any more questions because at that moment a Crown Victoria rolled into the parking lot and an older man got out. The two officers exchanged glances. Mack could read the look. *What's the chief doing here?*

The man greeted his officers, nodded in Mack and Hope's direction and said, "I'll take over here."

Mack could tell the female officer wanted to argue but she kept her mouth shut. Both of them walked away.

"I'm Chief Anderson," the man said.

Mack stuck out his arm. "Mack McCann. Thank you for coming."

The chief shook his hand, then Hope's. He glanced down at her knee. "Ms. Minnow, are you injured?"

"Bruised knee. A couple cuts. Nothing serious," Hope said.

"Do you want to sit in my car?" he asked.

Hope started to shake her head. "Yes," said Mack. It would make their conversation more private and it would provide protection for Hope in the event that somebody was crazy enough to try to take a second shot. "She needs some ice for her knee," Mack added.

"It's fine," Hope said.

The chief held up a finger. Then he walked over to where his officers were gathered around their vehicle. One of them opened the trunk and fiddled around with something inside. Then the chief was walking back with a cold bag.

He cracked it in the middle and handed it to Hope.

"Thank you," she murmured.

She was embarrassed. Mack didn't care.

The chief led them over to his car. The vehicle had warmed in the few minutes that it had been sitting in the sun. He started the engine to get the air conditioner going. He and Mack took the front seat, Hope a spot in the back.

"What the hell happened here?" Chief Anderson asked.

"I'm not sure," Mack said. "We were inside for maybe ten minutes. We came outside and got about thirty feet from the door before the shot was fired. Based on the sound and the damage to the window, I'd say it was a rifle. I believe it came from either the gray van or blue SUV that I previously described."

"You're right about the weapon," the chief said. "I heard from one of my officers on the way over. The bullet hit a display rack. We've recovered it. Not sure about where it came from. Other witnesses have also described the two vehicles but nobody got a license-plate number on either one. I've got an officer checking to see if there were cameras in the lot."

"What about street cameras?"

"Not here. This is usually a quiet community, Mr. Mc-Cann. Hard to get the city council to agree to spend that kind of money. Do you think this has anything to do with the notes that Reverend Minnow received?"

Mack knew it was possible that he and Hope had merely been in the wrong place at the wrong time. But he didn't think it was likely. The shot had been aimed at Hope. He was confident of that. By some stroke of luck, she'd bent down to get the rock out of her sandal.

That had saved her life. Maybe their baby's life.

"I don't know. I know that Hope and I were not followed to the store. I guess it's possible that somebody saw her inside."

The older man rubbed a hand across his jaw. "Mr. Mc-Cann, I don't normally invite victims to participate in the investigation, but Reverend Minnow shared some of your background with me. I think, in this case, it might be helpful. Do you want to come with me when I talk to the store manager?"

"Definitely. Hope comes, too," he added. He wasn't letting her out of his sight. He got out, opened the back door and held out a hand.

She took it.

Her touch was warm and it reminded him of how close he'd come to standing over her cold, dead body. He wanted to pull her tight, to hold her close, but he knew now wasn't the time. "Bring your ice," he said. "We'll get you a chair inside."

He positioned her between him and the chief as they walked into the store. There was glass on the floor and the display that the bullet had hit was pretty much trashed. Other than that, the store looked fine. They'd be back in business once they could get the window repaired and the glass swept up.

It didn't take them long to figure out some of what had happened once they spoke to the manager. "I'm dreadfully sorry," he said, mostly looking at Hope. "Jane, my cashier, did something that she should not have. She Tweets," the man added.

"What did she Tweet?" Mack asked, already having a pretty good idea.

"Your picture. We have a security system that takes still shots of everybody who walks in the door. She downloaded the picture, Tweeted it, and within minutes, it evidently got picked up by one of those online news agencies and retweeted." Now the man turned his glance to Mack.

"The text that went along with the picture was 'Hope Minnow and a sexy stranger.'"

"Double *S*," Hope murmured.

Chief Anderson and the store manager looked at her oddly. Mack smiled at her. He wasn't a stranger. Hope might want to delegate him to that role but he wasn't having any of that. Sexy? As long as she thought so.

"You'll follow up?" Mack asked the chief.

"Yes. I've got somebody on my staff that's really good at this kind of thing."

Mack was really good at it, but he couldn't take the time away from Hope to sift through all that data. "Okay. You can reach me on my cell."

He and Hope walked out of the store. There was no sign of Jane. Maybe she was off somewhere disabling her social-media accounts. There was, however, a photographer who snapped a picture.

Mack started to reach for the camera, intending to shove it down the man's throat.

"Hey, Hope," the man said, stepping back fast. "Making news again?"

"Byron," Hope said, a resigned note in her voice. "Long time," she added.

"Slow news day. This will help."

"Great. Mack, this is Byron Ferguson. He's a reporter with the local paper. Byron, this is Mack McCann. He's a family friend."

On to the *F*'s. Mack realized what she was doing. She was laying out the facts, trying to make it a nonstory.

"Family friend?" Ferguson repeated. "Not what I hear. I heard he's a bodyguard. That your family has received threatening letters and that you're the target."

Mack was going to wring somebody's neck. "We don't

have any comment," he said coolly. He cupped his hand underneath Hope's elbow.

The man moved with them. "Somebody took a shot at you today, Hope. Do you have any comment on that?"

Hope shrugged. "I think you're reaching for a story and you're a better journalist than that. Somebody shot at the window of the store and I just happened to be in the way."

"I wonder if that's what the police will say," Byron challenged.

They might, if the guy talked to Chief Anderson. The man would understand the family's hopes to downplay the situation.

"Let's go," Mack said. Even once they were past the reporter, Mack could hear the soft click of the man's digital camera.

He had no doubt that he and Hope were going to be front-page news tomorrow.

Chapter Sixteen

"That was more than a lucky guess. He knew about the letters. About you," Hope said under her breath as they walked to the car.

"Appears that way," Mack replied, disgusted. "You and I didn't tell him, your parents and Bing are all out of the country, and Mavis is out of town. That's everybody except for Chief Anderson."

"Maybe the chief gave something away when he walked over and talked to his officers. He probably felt as if he had to give some kind of explanation about why he'd suddenly showed up at the scene."

"You could be right. And then one of his officers let something slip to the reporter. Either on purpose or accidentally."

"I guess in the big scheme of things, it doesn't really matter whether people know about the letters or think I have a bodyguard or not."

"It would be better if people didn't know," Mack said.

"Well, we can't do much about it now."

"I'm going to have a conversation with Chief Anderson about it," Mack said, setting his jaw.

Hope almost felt sorry for the man. "Oh, my gosh, look at that," she said, thankful for something else to talk about.

They had reached Mack's car and the coffeepot, still in its sack, was sitting on the trunk of the car. Someone had been thoughtful enough to put it there. She opened the lid of the box. "It's fine. Nothing broke. We need to take it to Serena."

Mack looked like he wanted to argue. But he didn't. "I guess we can," he said. "She's going to wonder what took us so long."

"Maybe not. I think she has a program on her smartphone that tracks the police-scanner activity. She was using it the other night when I walked into the break area. She probably heard that there was an incident in the parking lot at Tate Drugs. I better call her, she'll be worried."

"I'm going to want to talk to Wayne," Mack said.

"Why?"

"Because he's got a reason to have a grudge against you. You're helping his wife to leave him."

"Not me. Paula." She started to pull her disguise back on. The pants, the shirt, the shoes. Finally, the wig.

"Maybe he knows you're one and the same."

"I don't see how." She knew it was a useless argument. If Mack had decided it was important to talk to Wayne, then he was going to talk to him.

"I'm also going to want to talk to your ex."

"Wills is not trying to kill me."

"Does he have a gun?"

"Several. He went hunting with his father."

"Is he a good shot?"

"I have no idea. He acted like he was. But then again, he acted as if he was good at everything. I know that wasn't true."

He gave her a look and she could feel the warmth spread from her chest to the tip of her head. Was he thinking that she was referring to Wills's prowess in the bedroom? Had she been? She'd commented on Serena's immaturity earlier. How mature was it to compare lovers?

There'd been no comparison. When Mack had left her bed this morning to go into the bathroom, her body had still been humming with the sweet afterglow of two really wonderful orgasms. He'd been a considerate lover, yet demanding. Gentle, but just rough enough to quickly bring her to a feverish pitch. Slow at the right times, yet very fast when it mattered. He'd evoked responses from her body that quite frankly had scared her.

Then he'd returned to the bed for the oops-the-condom-broke conversation, and she'd decided she was never having sex again.

Even as she'd been saying it, she'd known it was a damn shame.

"We're here," she said, stating the obvious as he pulled into Serena's lot. "I'll just run this in." She needed some air, even if it was hot, humid air.

He shook his head. "Call her. Tell her that I'll stick it inside by the front door." He got out, flipping the locks, even though he'd parked within fifteen feet of the door.

If he'd been hard to shake before, he was going to stick like glue now. She had to admit, she might not be all that eager to get rid of him. Hearing that window break had been horrific. Knowing that the bullet would have hit her had been terrifying.

When the paramedic had been checking her vital signs, she'd almost admitted that she felt sick, that she was awfully afraid that she was going to throw up. But those several minutes when she'd been receiving first aid had given her a chance to regroup, to catch her breath.

There was no proof that the bullet had been aimed at

her. And she'd tried to hang on to that thought the entire time they'd been talking to the police and the store manager. She'd done a pretty good job of it. It had gotten her through the ordeal.

Now she really just wanted to go home and cry.

Mack returned to the car and opened the door. He slid into the seat and looked at her.

"What's wrong?"

Ten minutes. That's all she had to last. "Nothing." She turned her face to the window.

"What happened? Did someone call?" He grabbed her phone, looked at it, searching for calls.

"No one called," she protested.

"Then what's wrong?" he demanded. He reached out and felt her forehead. "You're cold. I'm taking you to the hospital. You're in shock."

She pulled away from him. "I've been sitting here in front of the air-conditioner vent. I am not in shock."

He did not look convinced. She was sixty seconds from a visit to the emergency room.

"Listen, you idiot. If you want the truth, I was sitting here thinking about the fact that I almost died today. I don't want to die. I'm too young to die." Her voice cracked but she kept going. "And if I am pregnant, I didn't want my baby to die. I want to hold her in my arms. I want to teach her how to color and play with her in the park. I want to walk her to her first day of kindergarten and help her with her fifth-grade science project. I want it all, and today…today it almost ended. And I would have had none of it."

Then the dam broke and the tears that she'd believed could be held off another ten minutes came in a rush.

And she did not resist when he pulled her close and

held her. She cried hard, her face pressed to his chest, his hand stroking her hair. She cried until she could not cry anymore, until her body was spent with emotion. Only then did she lift her head.

And then he gently took the pad of his thumb and brushed away the tears that lingered on her cheeks and he kissed her forehead.

"I'm sorry," she said. Even when her ex-husband had beaten her and through their subsequent divorce, she hadn't cried that hard.

"You don't have anything to be sorry for. It's been a tough day. Let's go home," he said.

Home. Her home for now. But not necessarily for long. Weeks ago she'd started looking online for jobs, had actually applied for one. It wasn't exactly what she'd done before—she accepted that she'd already had her dream job, now she just needed work.

The company had called her the day before Mack had arrived to set up an interview. If it panned out, she was going to have some decisions to make. If not, well, maybe she could get an apartment down the hall from Serena. Two formerly battered women, trying to get their lives back on track. She'd have to tell Serena the truth about her identity—no way was she wearing Paula's ugly clothes forever.

Except it would be much easier to hide a pregnancy in them.

Good Lord, what was she going to do if she were pregnant? She'd need a very good job because it wouldn't be just her that she needed to provide for.

She'd need a job that offered flexibility and maternity leave and one that had good health-insurance benefits. Things could get more complicated quickly.

What was it that Mack had said earlier, something

along the lines of "sometimes we make things more complicated than they need to be"?

Yeah, well, he wasn't the one who was going to have a traveling companion for nine months.

And for the first time since they'd had the awkward *oops* conversation, she didn't break out in a cold sweat at the thought of being pregnant.

She would handle it. She could handle it. These last several years had proven to her that she could handle a whole lot.

Like getting shot at.

The thought of that had her shaking her head. The things you worry about in life were rarely the things that happened. It was a good lesson in worrying less.

"What are you thinking about?" Mack asked gently.

"I'm hungry," she lied. "I didn't eat breakfast or lunch and my stomach is letting me know. It's my turn to cook tonight."

He put the car in Drive and pulled out of the lot. "What's on the menu?" he asked.

"Chicken enchiladas. I know you've got a high standard of comparison, but I'm willing to see how mine stack up."

"Confidence. I like it." He drove for another few minutes.

I like it. Who would have thought three simple words would make her insides heat up? Her crying jag had left her vulnerable. That was the only explanation.

Was she willing to admit that she liked the idea of cooking him dinner? Of chatting with him while they sipped margaritas and snacked on chips and salsa? Of making sopaipillas for dessert and taking the warm fried dough, dripping with honey, up to bed with them?

Of licking honey off his wonderful body.

Having him lick if off her.

She turned the vent toward her face, which was very warm.

No, she was definitely not willing to admit that.

There wasn't going to be any licking, not of plates or bodies. Maybe some gnashing of teeth due to sexual frustration but that was it. They'd made a mistake last night and slept together. And time would tell if there were lasting consequences from that lapse. They didn't need to compound it and make it worse by doing it again.

She owned the lion's share of the blame for last night. She'd admitted that to Mack. She could be stronger. She would be stronger.

This was temporary duty for him. For her, a brief interlude before the rest of her life started.

He pulled into her driveway. "Let me go in first," he reminded her when he'd stopped the car.

She opened her door. "I want to check on Fred and his new family," she said. She grabbed the bag of cat food from the sack.

He rolled his eyes. "Okay. We'll go there first."

They walked into the barn, with Mack leading the way. There was nobody inside but Mama Kitty and her babies. Hope didn't try to touch any of them. She simply ripped open the sack and dumped some food on the cement about three feet away.

"Fred's AWOL," Mack said, stating the obvious.

"He'll be back," Hope said confidently. "He'll be a good daddy."

Mack's eyes heated up and she regretted the offhand remark. Was he thinking that he'd make a good daddy, too?

She didn't doubt that. And while she'd been very serious when she'd told him that she never intended to marry again, she would never keep a child away from the father. They would figure out a way to work through the logistics of having parents in different states. People did it all the time.

They walked out of the barn and toward the house. "I don't think your father is going to be crazy about more cats," he said.

She shrugged. "I'm going to be moving out soon. Maybe I can take one with me. I'll try to find a home for the other two."

"Moving? Where?"

"Not sure yet," she said. She waited while Mack unlocked the front door. "But it's time. I've never lived anywhere but the east coast. I imagine I'll stay in this region."

He stared at her, likely remembering his promise that he wouldn't bring up the subject of pregnancy, but also probably wanting to know whether a pregnancy would make a difference to her decision. But he stayed true to his promise and didn't force the topic. Instead, he simply opened the door and turned off the security system. "Stay here," he said. "If you hear anything unusual, get the hell out."

Before she might have been tempted to roll her eyes, much like he'd done when she'd demanded to see the kittens, but now she simply nodded and waited like a good girl.

He took the steps quickly. She didn't hear his footsteps on the old floorboards or hear any doors squeak as they were opened. Yet, she knew he was doing a thorough search.

Mack McCann had a nice touch at things.

Boy, did he.

He came down the steps. "Listen, I've been thinking.

Maybe it would be a good idea if you simply got out of town for a while. I have someplace you could go."

Now he had her curious. "Where?"

"You said that you've never lived anywhere besides the east coast. I'm giving you an opportunity to explore another state. I'd like you to go to Colorado with me. There's a place in the mountains, a cabin. Actually, two cabins. One was recently damaged in a fire and we're rebuilding that. The other cabin, which belongs to a friend, is available. We could go today."

"I can't go to Colorado," she said. What was he thinking?

"Why? You'll be safe in Colorado," Mack challenged.

"I have an interview in New York in three days, on May ninth. I have to stay here."

"An interview? Nobody told me anything about an interview."

"I'm sorry. I hadn't told anybody. I got the call just a few days ago. I applied for a position at a nonprofit in Brooklyn that supports after-school art programs in low-income areas."

He considered her. "It's not the Met," he said finally.

"No, it's not," she said lightly.

And while she might miss doing the work that she'd done there and having the responsibility, what bothered her most was that if she moved back to the city, she'd probably have to give up her volunteer work at Gloria's Path. It had been her salvation for the past year and, quite frankly, had kept her in Weatherbie these last couple of months, even when she'd been confident that her mother was well on the road to recovery.

She wasn't going to Colorado, she wasn't going back to the Met. The only place she was headed to was the kitchen. "I'm going to start the enchiladas," she said.

Chapter Seventeen

While Hope was busy making enchiladas, Mack called Chief Anderson. The man was friendly enough until Mack told him that he suspected that one of his officers had leaked information to the reporter.

"That's impossible," Chief Anderson said. "I understand you're a friend of the Minnow family, but I certainly don't appreciate those kinds of accusations."

"The reporter had information that had to have come from a knowledgeable source."

"And I'm telling you that he didn't get it from me or from one of my officers."

Mack didn't know whether he believed him or not, but there was little to be gained by continuing to harp on it. If they had leaked the information, they'd be more careful in the future. If not, well, then, Chief Anderson had a right to be pissed at Mack's accusations.

"I need to run some errands," Mack said. "I don't want to leave Hope unprotected."

"I'll come myself. And if it makes you feel any better, Mr. McCann, I won't tell anybody what I'm doing."

Mack hung up and went to find Hope. She was chopping onions on a cutting board.

"I talked to Chief Anderson. He says the leak didn't

come from him or his officers, that your reporter friend got it from someone else."

"First of all, Byron Ferguson is not my friend. I don't think he's necessarily my enemy, either, but that's neither here nor there." She tapped her knife on the butcher-block cutting board. "You know, there is another possible explanation."

"What?"

"Maybe my father gave Byron the information before he left town."

"What? Why?" Mack asked, shaking his head.

"Publicity. It's not a four-letter word and generally not considered a sin. Even if it was, I don't believe that would dissuade my father from pursuing it."

"I don't know," Mack said. "I just don't see him doing that."

Hope shrugged and started noisily chopping her onions again.

Mack put his hand up to still the noise. "I need to leave for a little while. Run some errands. Chief Anderson will be here while I'm gone. I want you to tell him about Gloria's Path."

She held the knife suspended in the air. "That doesn't seem like a great idea. The police don't appear to be able to handle sensitive information well. Plus, I'm not sure if you picked up on it or not, but the female officer today showed some overt animosity toward me. Not everyone on the force may have my best interest at heart."

He nodded. "You may be right. But the chief and his officers are what we have to work with right now. At least if the chief knows and something comes up during the course of the investigation that is connected to Gloria's Path, he won't dismiss it. I want you to tell him about Paula."

She stared at him. "I'll tell him about Paula and Gloria's Path," she said finally, "but I'm not going to tell him what led me there."

"It would be helpful if the police knew the truth about your ex. They would want to talk to him."

"It's enough that they know I have an ex-husband. That should automatically put him on the list. I don't need to air all my dirty laundry."

"You know, it's a crime to deliberately thwart a police investigation by keeping evidence a secret."

"I don't care."

Mack ran his hands through his hair.

"I don't know what you're upset about," Hope said. "Heck, people are Tweeting that you're a sexy stranger. I, on the other hand, have people disliking me before they even know me." She gave the onion a deliberate slice.

"It happens all the time. We judge people by the color of their skin, their ethnicity, their socioeconomic status, their marital status, everything."

"It's wrong."

"It is. We can't control that. About all we can control is giving Chief Anderson information that may be helpful to him. Trust me on this. I'm going to make sure that he understands that he needs to investigate anybody who might have a bone to pick with your father."

"It's so ironic," she said. "Someone is mad at my father and they want to take it out on me. Hell, *I'm* mad at my father. What do I need to do? Take an ad out in the newspaper and let this crazy know that they're not alone?"

"Maybe it's really you they're mad at."

"Me?"

"We can't discount that someone is deliberately trying to lead us down a dead-end path. I need you to tell

Chief Anderson the names of any person who might be upset with you or want to cause you trouble."

She rubbed between her eyes. "In fifth grade, I stole a two-dollar ring from the drugstore and I let my friend take the blame. She got grounded for a week. Does that count?"

"Put it on the list," he said, making sure she understood that he wasn't budging on this.

She shook her head. "Errands to run? You don't have any dry cleaning to pick up or banking to do. You're going to go see Wills. Aren't you?" She laid her knife down.

"You're damn right I am. And if I have any reason to believe that he has anything to do with this, I'm not going to be responsible for keeping anybody's secret."

WILLIAM BAYLOR THE THIRD answered the door wearing old running shorts, a T-shirt that used to be white and a sweatband around his head.

His mouth fell open when he saw Mack. "Oh. I thought you were the delivery guy. I ordered Chinese."

"No fortune cookies anywhere on me," Mack said. "I need a minute." He stepped forward, forcing *Wills* to take a step back.

The house was nice, but it didn't feel like Hope. It was too formal, with stiff-looking furniture and lots of dark wood. It was a large, two-story Colonial, way too big for a single guy.

"Look, I'm kind of busy," Baylor said.

"You don't look busy. You know what you look like? A wife beater. That's right. Some ass who decides to beat up somebody half his size just because he can."

Baylor's ruddy complexion turned a dull gray to match his shirt. "I don't know what the hell Hope told you, but if you think you're going to malign my good name, you've got another thing coming. I'll ruin you."

"I want to know what the hell you were doing between two and three o'clock today."

Baylor frowned at him. "I don't have to tell you anything. Just because you're screwing—"

Mack shoved him up against the wall, pinning him there, with his feet dangling in the air. "Shut up," he said. "Between two and three."

"I was at work. At the church. In a meeting with the administrative staff. There are eight people who can verify it."

Mack let him hang for another few seconds before he lowered him down. And then just for principle, Mack shoved him hard enough that Baylor's head snapped back and hit the wall.

"Get out of my house," Baylor said, his voice cracking at the end.

"If I have any reason to believe that you're causing one bit of trouble for Hope, you'll answer to me," Mack said.

He left without letting Baylor get the last word in. He intended to give Chief Anderson the vanilla version of this exchange and ask him to make sure that Baylor's alibi held water.

Maybe he was visible to those eight people at the meeting because he'd somehow discovered that Hope was going to be in that parking lot at that time and knew he'd need a strong alibi. Maybe Baylor had hired somebody else to do his dirty work.

It was a stretch, he had to admit, but if his visit had served no other purpose than to put Baylor on notice that he was being watched, it was worth it. And it had felt damn good to push Baylor around.

Mack keyed Wayne Smother's address into his GPS.

When he got there, there was no car parked in front of the small, frame-sided ranch and there was no garage. He rang the doorbell, then knocked. No answer. He walked around behind the house, through the small overgrown yard, and knocked on the back door. He heard a noise behind him and whirled.

"He's not home," said a woman wearing a big gardening hat, a long-sleeved shirt and jeans. "At about ten this morning, I saw him put a suitcase in his trunk. I told him last week I was going to report him to the city if he didn't mow his grass. I called them right after he left."

"Any idea where he might be going?" Mack asked.

"I have no idea. I think he has family in Texas. Not sure where. I'm trying to sell my house and it's not helping that this eyesore is in my backyard."

He didn't think it would help if he told her he really didn't care. He wanted to know where Wayne had been this afternoon. He pulled a business card out of his pocket. "Will you call me if you see him come back?"

"I guess. Can you make him cut the grass?"

"You call me and I'll cut the damn grass if I have to."

WHEN HE GOT back to the house, Hope was finishing the chicken enchiladas and Chief Anderson was enjoying a cup of coffee and some cookies. They both looked relaxed.

That made the knot in his stomach loosen just a little.

"Hi," he said. "Everything okay?"

"Very good," Chief Anderson said, then wiped his mouth with a paper napkin. "I appreciate you encouraging Hope to tell me about her volunteer work at Gloria's Path. Good organization, by the way. And helpful to know about Hope's connection to clients and their families. She's confident that nobody knows her as Hope Minnow, but still, it's good to have the information."

"I went to see Hope's ex-husband, William Baylor the third," Mack said, helping himself to a cookie from the plate on the counter.

The chief shook his head. "I know earlier today I invited you in to hear some witness reports. That wasn't an open invitation for you to start investigating the case."

"I wasn't waiting for an invitation. He says he was in a meeting with staff members this afternoon. I'd like that alibi to be verified."

"It will be. But do yourself a favor. Reverend Minnow said you were hired to provide extra protection for Hope. Why don't you concentrate on that and let us concentrate on getting the bastard who is doing this."

He wasn't going to make any promises he couldn't keep. "I'll try to keep out of your way, Chief, as long as I'm confident that you and your officers are doing everything they can to figure out who is behind these threats and the shooting today."

"We will. Don't worry about us." And with that, he got up and walked out the front door.

Mack sat down on one of the counter stools. "It's hard to have a lot of faith in a man with cookie crumbs on his face."

Hope smiled. "A cook takes that as a compliment. My cookies were so good that he was inhaling them."

"The cookies are good," he admitted. "How are the enchiladas coming?"

"So far, they appear to be right on track. Dinner will be ready in about an hour."

"Need some help?"

She looked surprised. "I guess. Do you know how to make guacamole?"

"Avocados, tomatoes, onions, salt. Lime or no lime?"

"Lime," she said, frowning at him.

"Jalapeños?"

"Un poquito," she said, pinching her fingers together.

"Sí, *senorita*. I'll merely wave the pepper over the dish."

MACK'S GUACAMOLE WAS GOOD, the enchiladas were some of her best work yet and the margaritas, well, they were stellar. Maybe, just maybe, because she'd come close to never having the chance to enjoy another margarita. Perspective made tequila sweeter.

She and Mack had dinner on the veranda. He'd lit several lanterns and found a television channel that played Mexican music. He'd put a speaker on the porch and she was now tapping her toes to "La Bamba" by Ritchie Valens, who had been dead long before she was born.

Mack pushed his chair away from the table. "That was so good," he said. "Seriously, your enchiladas have now taken first place. I'll be back once a week for eternity."

She picked up her glass and saluted him. Then she carefully set the glass down. "Have you spoken to my father about what happened this afternoon?"

"Not yet. Our agreement was that I would email him at night. I've done that the last couple of nights already."

"I'd appreciate it if you wouldn't tell him what happened today. I don't want them to worry."

"Them?" Mack queried. "Not just your mother?"

"Them. Her. Look, I'm still not convinced this is all real."

"You didn't hear the glass break behind you today when the bullet shattered it?"

She waved a hand. "That's not what I meant. Of course today was real. But the bullet may have not been aimed at me. It could have been a random shooting. Maybe the shooter wasn't even trying to hit anything. He or she was just out screwing around."

"This is not a game," Mack said.

"I know that. But if you tell my father what happened today, and he tells my mother, and she insists upon coming home, I'm never going to forgive myself. Please."

He nodded. "For now," he said grudgingly. "I'll keep it to myself for now, but I'm not making any promises into the future."

"Fair enough," she said. "By the way, I finally heard from Mavis today. She called while Chief Anderson was here. Her brother-in-law is holding his own. He had bypass surgery and is going home tomorrow. She'll be gone for a few days yet."

"Did you tell her what happened?"

"Absolutely not. She has enough to worry about. She lives to take care of others."

He picked up her plate, then his. "My turn for KP. Are you going to stay outside?"

"For a little while," she said.

"Okay. Please don't leave the veranda without telling me. No chasing after Fred if he happens to make an appearance," he added, trying to keep it light.

"Agreed," she said. She sat back in her chair and watched the lights dance over the pool water. She appreciated that Mack hadn't brought up her crying jag again. Nor had he belabored the points that she'd spewed out in her sudden need to make him understand why she was crying.

She'd basically admitted that she wanted a baby. She put her hand on her flat stomach. She'd ask him not to mention it again, but it didn't keep her from thinking about it. As delicious as the margaritas had been, she'd sipped just a little of hers, conscious of the fact that alcohol wouldn't be good for a baby.

Would her child be a blonde like her or a brunette like Mack? As a teenager, she'd yearned to have anything but blond hair and blue eyes. It was so boring. She'd wanted to be exotic, to have smoky dark eyes and hair so black that it almost looked blue.

Mack had dark hair and dark eyes.

Would her child be short or tall? She was just an average height for a woman but Mack was pretty tall.

The possibilities were endless.

But it was probably a whole lot of speculation about nothing. She wasn't pregnant. She was going to have her period next week and she'd be making jokes about escaping another bullet.

After about ten minutes, Mack came back out to the veranda. By then she'd moved to a lounge chair, closer to the pool.

He had a dish towel over one shoulder. "All done," he said. He pulled out a chair and sat.

It was a beautiful, warm spring night and the big trees and the soft lighting around the pool made it seem as if they were in a cocoon, separate from the real world, where windows got shot out and secrets got shared.

She closed her eyes. She could feel him beside her.

Watching over her.

And she felt safe.

"HEY, SLEEPYHEAD," he said, his voice very close, very soft. She opened her eyes. "You fell asleep," he said. "I didn't want to scare you, but I also didn't want you spending the night out here." He was leaning over her, his arms on the side of her lounge chair.

She stretched her arms over her head, and realized it

was a mistake when his eyes followed the movement of her breasts. His look was hot and hungry and it caused the need that she'd managed to hold at bay all day to surge forward.

It was crazy. They were both adults. Both single. The sex had been wonderful.

She reached up to touch his jaw. She felt the roughness of new beard. She ran the pad of her thumb over his bottom lip.

He held himself perfectly still.

She ran her tongue across her own top lip. His eyes followed the movement.

"Sometimes I'm hasty," she said.

"I'm listening."

"And I say things I regret," she said softly.

"Uh-huh," he said. He turned his face and kissed the palm of her hand.

The heat shot straight down her center. "Mack," she whispered.

He moved his mouth, traveling up the length of her arm. He licked the inside of her elbow, kissed her biceps, nuzzled her shoulder. Then his mouth found the delicate skin of her earlobe. "What did you say that you regret?" he whispered.

She was on fire. She turned her head, found his lips and they kissed. It was wet and sensual and she knew that she was not nearly as strong as she needed to be.

"That I wasn't going to sleep with you again," she admitted. "I take it all back."

She could feel the energy in his body. "Are you sure?" he asked.

"Yes," she said. Nothing had ever felt this right.

He gathered her up in his arms and carried her inside.

After kicking the door shut behind him and flipping the lock shut, he strode up the stairs.

He gently deposited her on the bed. The lights were off but the illumination from the yard light seeped through her sheer curtains. She could see the need on his face, could feel the heat radiating off his strong body.

"Make love to me," she said. "All night long."

Chapter Eighteen

Mack slept until nine o'clock, something rather unheard of for him. To be fair, he thought, as he grabbed workout clothes and tugged them on, he hadn't done all that much sleeping.

Which is why he was being very quiet. Hope was still asleep, lying on her side. Her naked body was wrapped in a sheet and her hair fell over her shoulder, as if sometime during the night she'd gathered it up and pulled it to the side.

He rubbed his fingers together, still able to feel the silkiness as he'd run his fingers through her hair when she'd bent over him and taken him in her mouth.

They'd used birth control every time and it had not failed. While they'd had no discussion about it, the knowledge that they might have been closing the gate once the horse was already out of the barn lingered in the back of his mind.

He'd been having sex for a good many years and never worried about an unplanned pregnancy. He'd been very careful. And it wasn't as if he'd been careless the other night.

Equipment malfunction. In the navy, that had the potential to take lives. Here, it had the potential to give life. It was a humbling thought.

He left the bedroom, walked downstairs, checked the alarm and did a quick look around the house. He glanced out the windows, surveying both the front and backyards. It was a beautiful morning.

And if Hope hadn't bent down to shake a rock out of her sandal, she might not be here to see it. The thought of that had him hitting the treadmill hard, pushing his body to the limit.

When he was finished, he walked upstairs. And just like she had been that first morning, Hope was sitting at the table, drinking a cup of coffee. She was not reading the paper this time. It was still folded up inside its plastic sack.

When he entered the room, she gave him a long, measured look that had his body temperature rising even higher.

"Good morning," she said. "If you're getting coffee, I'll take a refill."

He walked over to the counter, grabbed the pot and an empty cup and brought both back to the table. He refilled her cup first, then poured one for himself.

"Going to look at the paper?" he asked.

"I'm sort of afraid to," she admitted.

"How bad can it be?"

"Pretty bad. Byron Ferguson has a flair for the dramatic."

"Why is he so interested in you?"

"It's not just me. It's the whole family. And I'm not sure. I thought he'd tire of us. We really aren't that interesting."

Mack opened the paper. The headline wasn't good.

Hope Minnow Nearly Gunned Down

There was a picture of Hope and him, as they walked out of the store. It had to be one of those that he'd taken right as they saw him. The quality was good. Hope looked as beautiful as ever and Mack looked as if he wanted to bite somebody's head off.

Which proved the camera never lied.

He scanned the article. Some of it was fact: time and location of shooting, type of shell, amount of store damage. Then it got more sensitive. Family had recently hired a bodyguard after receiving threatening letters; everyone in the family was at risk; Reverend and Mrs. Minnow had chosen to leave town.

"This is not journalism," Mack said.

Hope shrugged. "It's what people like to read. It's scintillating. Probably sells a few papers."

Ferguson did not identify Mack by name in the piece. Which was odd, Mack thought, given that Hope had introduced him. Probably thought it made the piece more interesting to imply that he was some sort of mysterious bodyguard.

"He found out that your parents are out of town."

She shrugged. "That would have been easy. There are several people on my father's staff at the church. Any one of them could have innocently let it slip that he was out of the country."

She skimmed the article again. She looked up at him, shaking her head. "I know it's very immature of me, but I guess my biggest regret about this article is that Wills probably feels better about you, now that he knows you were hired to be with me."

Mack reached his hand toward her and cupped her chin. He gently tilted her face up. "Let's be really clear on this, Hope. I was not hired to *be with you*. What we have together is something very different. It doesn't have anything to do with what I was hired to do."

She stared at him. And for just a second, he thought she might be ready to have the what-if-I'm-pregnant conversation. But then she suddenly shoved her chair back and got up. "I have to change the date," she said, pointing to the calendar on the refrigerator. "Mavis always takes care of that. She keeps the rest of us on track."

Okay, they weren't going to talk. Now, that was. He was only going to let her put it off for so long.

Hope ripped off the page, wadded it up and threw it in the wastebasket, just as he'd seen Mavis do that the first morning. Muscle memory. As upset as the woman had been about her sister's news, she'd walked over and ripped off the top sheet, exposing the correct date. Probably because that's what she did every morning of her life.

He walked over to take a closer look and flipped through a couple pages. On Friday, May 9th, someone had written a note under the date. *Pick up symphony tickets.* "Somebody going to the symphony?" he asked.

Hope read it, too. "The junior college in Weatherbie has a nice little orchestra and my mother, who still plays the violin, is a big supporter. It's sort of a small-time operation. They don't have any administrative staff so they usually only offer advance tickets on one day. Otherwise, people get them at the window on the night of the show. My mother hates doing that."

Hope looked at the note closer. "That's Mavis's handwriting. She was probably planning on picking them up for Mom. That's the day of my interview but I can still take care of it."

"I'll bet you bought this calendar," he said.

She nodded. "Yes. How did you know that?"

He took his thumb and flipped through the pages.

"Every page has a picture of an animal in the corner along with some fascinating fact about them." He got close to the small print under the picture. "'Seals molt once a year. It can take up to six weeks.'" He smiled at her. "Fascinating."

She wrinkled her nose, dismissing his comment. "If it was up to me, I'd have a whole barn full of animals. Well, obviously not seals, but you get the idea. Horses, cows, chickens, dogs, cats. Bring it on. It's number three on my bucket list."

"What are numbers one and two?" he asked.

"Learn sign language and take a zip line across the jungle."

He laughed. "Sort of two extremes."

She shrugged. "Whatever. How about you? What's on your bucket list?"

"I don't have a bucket list."

She frowned at him. "Everyone should have a bucket list."

He snapped his fingers. "Okay. I've got one. To never be more than fifty yards away from a refrigerator with ice-cold beer."

She let out a huff of air and turned her chair so that her back was facing him. "I'm done with you," she said.

"Oh, no, you're not," he said. Then he scooped her off the chair, carried her upstairs and into the shower. "I just thought of something else," he said, right before he turned the water on.

FOR THE NEXT two days, things were about as perfect as they could be. They took turns cooking and Mack was a good student when she taught him how to make a pesto sauce using fresh basil. In turn, he helped her add biscuits and gravy to her repertoire. They watched movies on television, argued about whether the Colorado Rockies were a better baseball team than the New York Mets and they made love.

She tried not to think about the fact that in just days Mack would be leaving. He would go back to Colorado and she would do something, yet to be determined.

Neither of them talked about the possibility of pregnancy and they were very careful about using birth control. They did not talk about guns or reporters or threatening letters.

Mack may have read the paper. She did not.

On the morning of Friday, May 9th, she awoke to a beautiful day. The sky was bright blue and even though it was early, the temperature was already climbing toward the expected high of eighty.

"Breakfast," Mack said, walking into the room carrying a tray. "French toast and bacon. Coffee, too, of course."

She scooted up in bed. "It smells wonderful," she said.

He crawled in bed next to her, wearing just his underwear. They both grabbed a plate off the tray and started to eat. He'd warmed the syrup and put it in a small pitcher. She picked it up halfway through her meal to add a little more. It made her remember her honey fantasy.

"Why the smile?" he asked.

"Well, do you know what sopaipillas are?"

"Sure. Deep-fried dough with cinnamon and honey. Why?"

"I had this fantasy that we made sopaipillas, ate them in bed, and we dribbled honey over the other and licked it off."

His eyes lit up. "Really. You have lots of fantasies like that?"

"Maybe I have a few others. This particular one was very nice. Very sweet, as I recall."

He took her plate away from her.

"Hey," she said. "I wasn't done."

"Yes, you are." He pulled off his shorts and picked up the small pitcher. "Sometimes you just have to make do with what you got."

THEY WERE LATE getting out of bed and had to hurry to get ready. Hope's interview was at 1:30 p.m., so they wanted to leave the house by noon to ensure that they arrived in Brooklyn on time.

Traffic flowed pretty well and they were able to find a parking spot near the corner of Fifth Avenue and Ninth Street. "We'll need to walk from here," Mack said.

They found the building, took the elevator to the third floor and found the office. "You can't come in with me," she said. "It will look as if I was afraid to come to the job interview on my own, that I had to drag my boyfriend with me."

"Boyfriend," he repeated, smiling.

"I'm saying that's what their receptionist will think. And they'll mention it to the hiring manager and my name will be crossed off the list and they'll write some crazy notation in the margin like 'does not appear to be able to act independently,'" she said, making air quotes.

He studied her. "Fine. I'll walk you to the door and hang around in the hallway. You didn't tell anybody about this interview, did you?"

"No."

"Then there's no reason to think that there is any danger. I know we weren't followed. I made sure of that."

"There's a coffee shop just down the street," she said. "You could kill some time there."

"Don't worry about me. Are you nervous? You seem nervous."

She ran a hand through her hair. "Of course I'm nervous. I've only interviewed for a couple jobs in my entire life. I don't even know if I want this job, but still, I want them to want me. Does that make sense?"

"Sure. You want to be the one to say no. Not the other way around."

"Exactly. Okay, I'm going in." She opened the door.

"Hey," he whispered. "You're going to knock their socks off."

The door closed, separating her from Mack. She was smiling when the receptionist looked up.

"Good afternoon. I'm Hope Minnow." *And I'm here to knock your socks off,* she added silently.

"The director will be right with you," the young woman said, her hands still on her keyboard. "Please have a seat."

The waiting area looked a little bit like the one in Gloria's Path. Well, how Gloria's Path had looked before the fire. Which reminded her that she needed to check in with Sasha. She normally volunteered on Friday nights. It was usually a busy night. Probably had something to do with the fact that people had finished out their work week and decided to have a few drinks. Two drinks turned into four, sometimes six, and tempers became harder to control.

The clients were going to have to move out of the hotel tonight because of the soccer tournament. She needed to know where to show up for work.

Hope sat on the couch and picked up a magazine off the table. She put it back down. She didn't really want to read gossip about anybody else when her own situation was getting so much attention.

She was going to have to figure out a way to get Byron Ferguson off her back. He'd been helpful in the past, when the publicity had been uncomfortable for her father, but suddenly, that no longer seemed so important.

Was it possible that she was done being mad?

Certainly not done with being hurt. But anger was a pretty useless emotion. She'd known this for some time, of course, but within the past couple of days everything had gotten much clearer.

Getting shot at and falling in love had a way of doing that.

Oh, dear Lord, falling in love? She picked up the magazine and fanned her face, which was suddenly hot.

Was it possible? Had she really fallen in love with Mack McCann? No. It was just sex. And some good conversation. Nice dinners. Laughter.

Oh, no.

"Hope, the director will see you now."

MACK SAT FOR a while, then prowled the halls, never letting the office door out of his sight. Hope had been so nervous. It was the first time he'd seen her like that. It was sort of cute.

Hell, Hope would be cute wearing prison stripes, picking up garbage off the side of the road

He knew she'd do well in the interview. And if she got the job, what would that mean? She'd move back to the city, maybe even live in Brooklyn and be close to her work. He walked over to the window that was at the end of the hallway and looked out. It was a clear day. He could see quite a ways. Brooklyn didn't have the flash that Manhattan had. The buildings were older and there were more big trees. There were no skyscrapers.

Could he live here? He'd certainly lived in less attractive places over the past years. But his heart had been set on Colorado. He'd accepted the job with Matrice Biomedics so that he could stay there.

None of that mattered, he realized. What mattered was being where Hope was. And maybe, where their child was.

He'd live on the moon if that's what it took. But first he was going to have to convince Hope that this wasn't a temporary affair, that he was in it for the long haul. He was going to have to convince her to try marriage again.

He turned when he heard the office door open. Hope walked out, looking beautiful as usual, although more formal in her black dress and heels. She'd pulled her long hair up and pinned it in the back. He'd seen his sister do similar things with her hair. He remembered his father telling him that a woman's ability to style her hair was God's way of showing that women were the superior species. He wondered what Reverend Minnow would say to that.

"How did it go?" he asked.

"Okay, I think. They said they'd let me know. I'm just glad it's over with."

"Do you want to spend some time in the city? We could drive over to Manhattan."

She shook her head. "I need to get back to pick up the symphony tickets for Mavis. I'll bet you ten bucks that she's going to call and ask about them."

"If she remembers what she wrote on the calendar," Mack said, opening the door for Hope.

"Everything she writes on the calendar, she enters into her smartphone, too. She started doing that because she was out running errands once and came home, only to realize that she'd forgotten to do something that she'd written on the calendar. She had to go back out and she didn't like that. Like I said, superefficient."

The drive back to New Jersey didn't go as smoothly as the drive in. There was an accident on the highway and traffic was backed up for miles.

They were sitting still when Mack's cell phone rang. He looked at the number. "Chief Anderson," he said to Hope.

"Put it on speaker," she requested.

"McCann," he answered.

"It's Chief Anderson. I've got some news for you."

Chapter Nineteen

"I've got you on speaker," Mack said. "Hope is here."

"I figured as much. Anyway, this afternoon we arrested Wayne Smother on charges of attempted murder. We got a signed confession from him. He's the one who shot at you the other day. He's the one who sent the letters."

Mack looked at Hope. Her mouth was open.

Somehow Smother had connected Paula to Hope. Hope had been confident that only two people knew the truth—Sasha and Mavis. He could tell by the sudden distress in Hope's eyes that she'd just come to that same conclusion.

"How did he know that Hope and Paula were one in the same?" Mack asked.

"His wife, Serena, told him. She evidently recognized Hope the first time she met Paula but she didn't say anything. She was pretty impressed by the fact that her volunteer counselor was Hope Minnow and she told Wayne."

It fit. Serena and Wayne had a relationship where they were often trying to one-up the other.

"Smother was also responsible for the fire at Gloria's Path so there will be some additional, very serious charges against him and his friend, who evidently owns an old yellow El Camino. Serena suspected that Wayne was responsible for the fire but didn't tell anyone. In her own way, she didn't want to get her husband in trouble. In the end, however, she did the right thing. She read Byron Ferguson's story in the paper and called us, saying why she thought her husband might be responsible. We got a search warrant for his house and we found a notebook where he'd scribbled down the address of your father's office."

"Where did you find him?"

"He was staying with his friend who owned the El Camino. Serena led us in that direction. I think he was sort of glad we'd figured it out. It was almost as if he'd gotten himself into something that he couldn't get out of."

Hope leaned forward in her seat. "But the threats referenced the loss of a child. I don't think Wayne and Serena Smother had any children."

"You're right. He did that to throw suspicion in other directions. He didn't realize that your parents weren't aware of Paula. He figured once there were threats against you, they would demand that you stop volunteering at Gloria's Path. He thought you were talking Serena into leaving him. When you didn't stop volunteering, he decided he had to take it a step further. His wife getting her own apartment was the final straw."

"How did he know we were at that store?" Mack asked. He knew that he had not been followed from the apartment.

"Serena sent him a text, bragging about how nice her apartment was, how close it was to the train and how helpful everyone from Gloria's Path had been. So helpful in fact, that they were getting her a coffeepot at the store. He didn't know for sure where the apartment was, but he had a pretty good idea of the general area. He took a guess at which store and he got lucky. He said that he'd almost given up when he saw the two of you walking out of the store. He took it as some kind of sign."

"Has he posted bail?" Mack asked.

"Nope. And I don't think he'll be able to. He's going to sit in jail until his trial. Of course, that counts as time served."

"Will you let us know if he does make bail?" Hope asked.

The chief indicated he would. Mack didn't care. He'd put things in place to monitor Wayne Smother until the man was safe behind prison bars. The man would never, ever have a chance to get close to Hope again.

"The press is aware of the arrest," the chief said. "Ferguson has already interviewed Serena Smother. I'm afraid the truth about your volunteer work in disguise is no longer a secret. He called and asked me about it and I basically shut it down with a no-comment response. Unfortunately, he can be a bit of an ankle biter when he smells a story. I thought you should be prepared."

Mack looked at Hope. Her eyes were troubled and he suspected that she was wondering if the full secret would somehow unravel. Would Byron Ferguson give up until he knew what had brought Hope to Gloria's Path?

"Thank you," Hope said. "I appreciate knowing that. Can't wait for tomorrow's paper," she added drily.

The chief laughed. "That's how I feel every morning. Just try to remember, every news story blows over eventually."

"Of course," Hope said, not sounding confident. "Thank you, Chief. I do appreciate your assistance with everything."

"Well," the man said, suddenly sounding unsure, "I have admired your father for a long time. He's got to be very proud of you."

Hope smiled at Mack. "Yes. Yes, I'm sure he is."

"Thanks, Chief," Mack said quickly. "Let us know if anything else comes up."

"I will. I'm just glad it's over," the man said, and hung up.

They drove in silence for several minutes. Finally, she turned to him. "It really is over, isn't it?"

"Looks that way," he said.

She leaned her head back against the headrest. "I'm so sorry," she said.

That wasn't exactly the reaction he'd expected. "What for?"

"For not taking the threats seriously. You did. You were right. My family was right. I was just so busy being mad at my dad that I couldn't see anything else. I couldn't see the possibilities."

"You have a right to be mad. Keeping Baylor at the ministry was a big mistake. Your dad had to know that."

She smiled. "You know, earlier I told you that it didn't matter. And I was lying then. It did matter. But suddenly it really doesn't." She looked down at her hands. Then at him. "I owe you for that. I do."

"You don't owe me anything."

She smiled at him. "Let's agree to disagree."

"I think I should tell your parents what has happened. They deserve to know."

She nodded. "You're right. I'm sure they will be very relieved to know that the threat is over."

"But I'm not leaving, even if they tell me I can."

FERGUSON HAD LEFT three messages on the house phone's voice mail. He was working on a story for tomorrow's paper and he wanted to give her a chance to comment.

She listened to the first one and deleted the other two without listening.

"He's probably going to talk to other people who work at Gloria's Path," Mack said. "The truth about how you came to be a volunteer there may come out."

"It could," Hope admitted. "I don't think it will, however. Sasha is the only one who knows, but I don't think she'll tell him."

"Why?"

"Well, for one thing, she hates the local paper," Hope said, grateful to talk about something else. "Her ex-husband from her second marriage sells advertising for them. She hates the local car dealer, as well," she added, with a smile. "First ex-husband works there."

"Two exes. Bad luck or bad choices?"

"I don't know. Sasha was helpful to me at a time when I desperately needed help. And I think she's got a good attitude about things. She works at a nursing home, and while it can be a sad place, she finds fun in it. She's always talking about this one elderly man, Charlie Fenton, who manages to leave, without any of his clothes, because he's intent upon buying donuts for his girlfriend, who also lives there. Sasha is a good storyteller."

"Sounds as if you think she's a good friend, too. Are you going in tonight?"

"I usually do volunteer on Fridays, but I think I'll let Sasha know not to expect me for a couple nights. By then, some of the interest will die down. Ferguson may have found another hot story by then."

"In Weatherbie?" Mack asked.

"It's almost time for the seniors to be done with their classes for the year. Maybe we'll get lucky and they'll pull some good pranks that will get some attention. Goats loose on the track. Underwear up the flagpole."

"Got to love small-town America," Mack said, shaking his head. "So let me get this straight. You don't have any obligations tonight or into the foreseeable future?"

"Well, on Tuesday—the thirteenth—I have to cover Mavis's volunteer shift for the library fund-raiser. She said that she'll be back that day, but not until the evening."

"Okay," he said, "we can fit that in."

"Fit it in?"

Mack picked up his phone and started dialing.

"Who are you calling?" she asked.

"The pizza guy. We're sure as hell not cooking tonight, or tomorrow night, or any night until Mavis comes home."

"Oh, really?" she asked, her tone challenging. "I thought we were having fun cooking."

"It was fun. But comparatively speaking, there are other things I enjoy more."

"I wonder what that is?" she teased.

"Keep thinking," he said. "Let's see. Pizza tonight, then Thai, and maybe even gyros from the little Greek place on the corner."

She smiled at him. "You know I do love to support the local economy."

On Tuesday, at ten minutes before seven, she slipped out of Mack's arms. Of course, when he immediately sat up in bed, she realized he was already awake.

"Time to wash cars?" he asked, voice husky.

"Yes. I'm going to take a quick shower, grab something to eat and get over there."

He swung his legs over the bed and she found it difficult to take her eyes off of him. He was naked and so amazingly gorgeous. "We'll shower together," he said.

"Oh, no," she answered, already moving toward the bathroom door. "I'll be an hour late."

"But happy when we get there," he countered.

"We? You don't have to go. The threat is over, it will be perfectly safe."

"I want to go," he said. "I already checked today's paper. After running articles for two days, you'll be happy to know that Ferguson finally took a day off today. But still, people will likely be talking about what's happened. I don't want you to have to face that alone."

"At least Byron didn't dig too deep into the reasons I chose Gloria's Path."

"No, he didn't. I think he's a lazy journalist."

"I'm grateful for that. I'll have to be careful if he's there today."

"Don't worry. I'll handle him," Mack said.

She leaned in and kissed him on the cheek. "I'm a big girl, Mack."

"I know that. And capable as hell. It's just that Ferguson rubs me the wrong way."

She tossed her hair over one shoulder. "If he gets too nosy, I'll just hit him with the hose."

THE ORGANIZERS OF the car wash practically fell all over themselves when both he and Hope showed up. "I heard Mavis was out of town," the woman who was registering volunteers said, "so I thought we'd be one short."

"Mavis made sure it was covered," Hope said and accepted the stack of towels the woman handed her.

"That was a terrible thing that man tried to do," the woman said in a loud whisper.

"Yes, yes it was," Hope said, moving down the line to pick up sponges.

They joined the twenty or so other volunteers and then

divided to make three lines with someone spraying, a few people washing and several more drying.

The event was held in the parking lot of the library that was going to get all new windows if they could raise enough money. At one point, when Mack looked up from drying a car, and the line of cars stretched to the end of the block, he figured the building might get a new roof out of the day, too.

By noon, the temperature had hit eighty-eight. There wasn't a cloud in the sky. People were friendly and happy to donate twenty bucks for a free car wash.

"I need more towels," a woman in their group said.

"I'll get them," Hope said. She put down her hose and started walking toward the pallets at the far end of the parking lot, where extra supplies were stored. Ferguson had not shown up, but still Mack kept one eye on her as she crossed the lot and squatted down to pick up towels.

He saw her stand up.

But then she dropped her towels, put a hand to her forehead, and sank to the ground.

Chapter Twenty

The former cross-country star sprinted across the lot. And when he pushed his way past the four or five people who had already gathered around Hope, her face was pale and she was blinking fast.

"What happened?" she asked.

"I think you fainted," a woman said.

"Call 911," Mack said. He reached for Hope's wrist to check her pulse.

"No," Hope said. She smiled at the woman, offering reassurance. "I'm fine. Really. I think I just had too much sun."

"You fell on the pavement," Mack said. "You might have hit your head."

She shook her head. "I didn't. Really, Mack, I'm okay."

Well, bully for her, Mack thought, because he was a wreck. When she'd gone down, his first thought was that she'd been shot at again, and this time had been hit. His heart had stopped in his damn chest.

"Can I get you something to drink?" This from the woman who had given the fainting diagnosis.

"Thank you. Maybe some lemonade," Hope said.

"She'll drink it over there," Mack said to the woman. Then he scooped up Hope into his arms and carried her over to sit under the shade tree.

"Oh, good grief," Hope said. "Put me down."

He ignored her until they got to the grassy area where big oak trees provided lots of shade. Then he gently put her down. He sat next to her.

"What happened?" he asked.

"I'm not sure," she admitted. "I picked up the towels, stood up and suddenly, everything went gray to black. Fast. I've never fainted before. I don't like it."

"Me, either. You scared me," he admitted. "Are you sure you won't go to a doctor?"

She shook her head. "No. I don't think that's necessary. I just got too warm, maybe a little dehy—"

She stopped because the woman was carrying over two lemonades. She handed them each one. "Enjoy," she said and walked off.

Hope took a big drink.

"We'll take off once you finish that," he said.

"We can't leave. We have to finish the car wash."

"Oh, no. You're not finishing anything. You're done. The most pressing thing you need to do is finish your lemonade."

"But—"

"But nothing. I'll compromise. If you'll sit in the shade and drink your lemonade, I'll keep washing and drying cars. If you insist on helping, all bets are off."

She rolled her eyes. "Fine. Can I sit at the table and accept the money?"

"As long as the table is in the shade. And then we're going back to your house. And you're going to rest."

"I have a request," Hope said.

"I'm listening."

"I want you to go to the dinner tonight for Brody at the White House. I do. Your name is still on the guest list. You have plenty of time to take the train if you leave soon."

"I don't want to leave you. I could make a few calls, probably get you on the list."

She shook her head. "The media circus is somewhat controlled here. But at the White House, the story could get legs again and that's not fair to you."

"I can handle the media," Mack said.

She smiled. "You've proven that you can handle most anything. But you shouldn't have to. Just go. Please. Brody is one of your best friends. You're never going to have another chance to honor him in this way."

He'd been feeling badly that he was going to have to bail on Brody. But hadn't wanted to pressure Hope to go.

"Are you sure?" he asked.

"Yes. I'll be fine. Mavis will be back tonight and we'll hang out."

"I'll only be gone for a few hours. And I don't think I'll do the train. A plane will be faster. Then dinner for a couple hours and I'll be back before you know it."

"I know. Don't worry. The danger is over."

He knew that, but still, he'd come too close to losing Hope. "Your parents will be back tonight," he said.

"I know. I'm going to talk to my father. I need to understand his side of the story."

MACK HAD CONSIDERED taking a commercial flight to D.C., but decided that a small plane out of a private airstrip suited his needs better. It would reduce the amount of time he needed to be away from Hope even more.

Still, he'd been at the airport for less than twenty minutes and he was already missing her. He knew he should stop worrying. But he couldn't. He wanted to wrap her up in cotton and carry her around on soft pillows. Of course, she wanted none of that. She wanted to wash cars all day in the hot sun.

She and Mavis would be fine now that Wayne Smother was locked up. And Patsy and Archibald Minnow would be home late tonight.

He would no longer be needed.

Too bad.

He loved Hope and didn't intend to walk away. He understood why she was so nervous about getting married again. He could be patient, but he wasn't giving up.

He couldn't wait to tell Brody all about her. And when he felt the plane start to taxi down the runway, he knew that he'd be able to do just that in less than an hour. He was meeting his friend at the hotel. Then they would travel together to the White House for dinner.

He closed his eyes, hoping to catch a catnap. That thought had him smiling. Catnap. As in cat. He'd arranged to purchase Fred from the Websters. He knew he was playing dirty, but he didn't care. He was playing to win.

Forty-five minutes later, the wheels touched down and he was off the plane. He carried the tux that he had Chandler ship to him days ago, just in case. She was happy to do it, she'd said, because it gave her official permission to snoop in her brother's closet.

He hailed a cab and drummed his fingers on the door when they hit D.C. traffic and moved at a snail's pace. Finally, he was at the hotel. It was big and splashy with lots of marble in the lobby. He didn't care about that. He cared a whole lot when he spied Brody Donovan unfold his lean body from one of the couches.

Brody looked good. Tanned. Fit. There were some lines around his eyes that hadn't been there two years ago when Mack had last seen him. Of course, Brody had spent most of those two years on the front lines, working miracles for soldiers. That would tend to put a little wear and tear on the body.

Mack gave his friend a big hug. "Good to see you," he said.

"Glad you could make it," Brody replied. "Is your assignment in New Jersey all done?"

"Almost. Hope's parents return to the States late tonight."

"You managed to keep her out of jail. Good for you."

Mack pulled back. He knew Brody was kidding, but he couldn't let it go. "I'm going to marry her."

Brody squinted his eyes at him, assessing. "Damn. I think you're serious."

"As a heart attack. She's amazing, Brody. Beautiful and smart and fun. She's kind and thoughtful and giving. Oh, and she makes the best enchiladas."

"Well, then, get a license and get it done."

"I haven't gotten her to say yes yet."

Brody grabbed him by the elbow and started to drag him to the bar.

"What are you doing?" Mack said. "We have to get dressed and get going."

"Oh, no. I just learned that some woman has my best friend in knots. You can't drop a bombshell like that and think the conversation is over. Come on. I'm buying."

HOPE WAITED FOR twenty minutes after Mack left the house before she got in the car and drove to the drugstore. Fortunately, Jane wasn't working. Hope didn't recognize the clerk on duty.

She didn't care.

She bought two home pregnancy-test kits. For days

she'd been thinking about it. But this morning, the fainting episode had pushed her over the edge.

She'd told Mack the truth. She never fainted.

But she hadn't told him that she'd woken up feeling a little nauseous this morning. He wouldn't have left her side. And she needed to do this by herself.

When she got home, she went upstairs, read the directions and went into the bathroom. Then she repeated the test a second time.

Both results were the same.

Pregnant. With a capital *P*.

Hope Minnow was going to have a baby.

She felt like dancing around the room. But she didn't because she heard the security alarm go off and knew that Mavis had returned. She picked up all the trash, put it in a bag and then shoved it under her bed. She didn't want anybody seeing this.

Not until she'd had a chance to tell Mack. He deserved to know first. He'd be back by midnight at the latest. Eight hours. No big deal.

She took the steps to the first floor, laughing silently when she realized that her hand was hovering over the handrail. She'd been taking these steps for years and never considered using the handrail.

But now a fall might not impact just her. It was amazing how pregnancy changed one's perspective.

"Hey, Mavis," she said, entering the kitchen.

"Hi, Hope. I missed you," she said, giving her a hug. "I didn't see Mack's car."

"He's at an event honoring an old friend. In Washington, D.C. He'll be back late tonight. Probably about the same time as my parents. He figured it was safe to go now that Smother is in jail."

"Makes sense," Mavis said.

"How's your brother-in-law? And your sister?"

"Better."

"Glad to hear it. And glad that you're home. I'm going to go downstairs and walk on the treadmill for a while."

"Okay," Mavis said. "I bought stuff for Chinese for dinner."

"Perfect. I'll see you in a half hour."

WHEN HOPE CAME UPSTAIRS, she was surprised to see that the kitchen was empty. She looked through the French doors to see if Mavis was on the veranda. No sign of her.

"Mavis?" she yelled. A sense of foreboding traveled through her body. Mavis was always really good about telling her if she was leaving the house.

She reached for the house phone, intending to try Mavis's cell number. That's when she saw the note on the calendar.

Ran to the store—needed cornstarch. Will be back in a little while.

She realized that Mavis had put the note where she thought it was likely that Hope would see it. The woman wouldn't be gone long. Maybe she'd just sit outside and enjoy the late-afternoon sun while she waited for her.

She was just about to open the back door when she heard a cell phone ringing. It took her a minute to realize that it was Paula's phone that was still in her purse. She pulled it out, recognized the number as Gloria's Path and answered it. "This is Hope," she said, relishing the fact that she didn't have to hide her identify any longer.

"Hey, it's Sasha."

"What's going on? I heard you were out of town for a couple days."

"Had to visit my mom unexpectedly. She broke a hip."

"Oh, I'm sorry. Is she okay?"

"Yeah, except she's getting discharged from the hospital today. I really need to be there. However, we got a call on the hotline. There's a new client and I was going to pick her up. She's at the Smart Gas station, just east of town. A neighbor gave her a ride there."

"Is she okay?"

"Fine, now. She got out of the hospital two days ago after her husband knocked her around. She went home, but woke up this morning and decided that she wasn't going to take it anymore. Her name is Dana. Mid-forties. Short brown hair. I didn't want to tell her that there wasn't anyone available to meet with her. Jackie is willing to come in early but can't get there for a couple hours. Could you pick up Dana and get her settled at Gloria's Path? Jackie will relieve you as soon as possible."

She'd told Mack that she intended to stay home. "There's no one else?"

"No. I checked. I wouldn't ask if…"

It was true. Sasha had always demonstrated her willingness to take an extra shift or complete a dirty job. She never asked one of the volunteers to do what she wouldn't do. "Just for a couple of hours?" Hope asked.

"Definitely."

She would be home before Mack got done with his rubber chicken or whatever it was that they served at White House dinners.

"Okay. I'll do it. Good luck with your mom." Hope hung up the phone and picked up a pen. On the calendar, below Mavis's writing, she scribbled, *Need to help a client. Eat without me and I'll grab something when I get home.*

She grabbed her purse, grateful that she didn't have

to put on the ridiculous disguise anymore. She got into her car and secured her seat belt. Five minutes into her drive, her cell phone rang. She looked at the number. The school in Brooklyn. "This is Hope," she answered.

Ten minutes later, she pulled into the parking lot of Smart Gas. It was a locally owned gas station and did a big business with the trucks that lumbered through New Jersey on their way to New York City, as well as the commuters who burned through tanks of gas a week.

She did not see a lone woman standing outside. She parked in front of the convenience-store portion of the gas station and went inside. There were only three aisles. No women customers. Hope approached the cashier. "Hi. I was supposed to meet a woman here. Mid-forties. Short brown hair."

"I just gave her the key to the ladies room," the man said, pointing outside. He turned to help the next customer.

Smart Gas had been built thirty years ago, when gas stations had exterior entrances to their restrooms. It had remained in the Smart family for all these years and they'd evidently found no need to change that.

Hope went outside, walked down the length of the store, turned the corner and didn't see the man who stepped out of the shadows until it was too late.

He put a hand over her mouth and jerked her head backward. "Cooperate or you're dead," he said.

Chapter Twenty-One

The bar served a pretty good microbrew and Mack was happy enough to participate in a toast to his good fortune. He felt lucky as hell. He'd accepted this assignment never realizing that he was going to meet a wonderful woman, somebody that he would want to spend the rest of his life with.

"Have you told Chandler yet?" Brody asked.

Mack shook his head. "No way. I want to see her face. But I also don't want to impose upon her big day. I'll tell her afterward."

"Maybe she'd want a double wedding?" Brody suggested.

"If I throw a wrench into things and end up delaying Ethan and Chandler's wedding, I don't think I'll be around to enjoy my own. Ethan will get me for sure."

"It's so cool that Ethan and Chandler ended up together," Brody said, setting down his empty glass. "It's pretty amazing when you think about the chances."

"It is. Although, I don't know why I'm surprised," Mack said. "When I think back, he was always looking out for her. Always wanted to let her tag along."

Brody nodded. "He's come full circle. And I barely have a chance to get used to that news before my other best friend takes the plunge."

"You're next," Mack said, standing up. It was time for them to get to the White House.

"I don't think so," Brody said, dismissing the idea immediately. "What's next for me is a nice little vacation. I'm going to South America. Going to lie on a beach somewhere and enjoy ice-cold rum drinks."

"That sounds pretty good."

Brody slapped him on the back. "It sounds excellent. And there aren't going to be any bombs going off or bullets whizzing by. That sounds even better." He started walking. "Come on. I hate to make the president wait on me."

The two men dressed in Brody's room, with Brody in military dress and Mack in his tux. "You clean up pretty good," Mack said.

"Likewise. Although I expected it from you. An outcome of your James Bond genetic material."

"If you say things like that tonight, they're going to take back the award."

"Let 'em try."

Mack pulled out his phone. "I'm going to send a quick text to Hope." He typed in his message and hit Send.

The two men left the room and took the elevator downstairs. They exited the lobby, intending to walk the four blocks to the White House. Mack checked his phone three times on the way. Nothing.

"No response?" Brody asked, obviously picking up on his preoccupation.

"No."

"Maybe she's in the shower?"

"Maybe." He didn't think so. Hope had already showered once that day. He knew that because he'd showered with her. Who could have known that raspberry shower gel could be put to so much good use? They'd been in there so damn long that the hot water had run out.

There was no reason to think there should be any problems. But none of that logic did anything to settle the unrest that had lodged itself in his chest.

They walked the remaining two blocks. There was a small group of attendees waiting to get cleared by security. They took their place in line. As they shuffled forward, Mack once again pulled out his phone. He pressed Hope's number and listened to it ring. It went to voice mail. "Call me," he said quickly. It was their turn for security.

They showed identification and were allowed to pass through a set of electronic gates to complete the screening. Once past that, they were greeted by a woman at the door, wearing a long black dress. She escorted them to their seats in the State Dining Room.

People were milling around, taking seats, and there were servers floating through with trays of wineglasses. There was music playing in the background. It seemed everyone wanted a chance to meet Brody, to congratulate him on his service. He, in turn, introduced Mack.

It should have given Mack plenty to think about.

But all he could think about was Hope. And that his phone wasn't ringing.

He tried her again. Voice mail again.

He called the house. No answer there, either.

The president was approaching, shaking hands as he came. Mack searched through his numbers, found the one he needed and pushed Send. It was answered on the third ring. He explained what he needed, gave her the number of Hope's cell phone and hung up.

"Who was that?" Brody asked.

"Pam Brogan. Best data analyst I ever worked with. I'm tracking the location of Hope's cell phone."

Within two minutes, his phone was buzzing. He answered and felt the quick burn of panic spread across his chest. He clicked the end button just as the president stepped in front of them.

"Good to see you again, Mack," the man said.

"Thank you, sir."

The leader of the free world shifted his attention to Brody. "Dr. Donovan," he said. "It's a pleasure." The president went on to thank Brody for his service and said he admired both his skill and courage.

Once the president had moved on, Mack leaned into Brody and whispered in his ear. "I hate to do this. You are my best friend and I want to be here to see you honored. But I can't stay. Pam tracked the location of Hope's cell phone to the middle of a field. Something is very wrong."

"Let's go," Brody said.

"You can't go. You're one of the people getting honored."

Brody waved a hand. "There are three other honorees here. I shook the president's hand. That's good enough for me. You're my friend. If there's trouble, then I want to be there to help you. But you have to do one thing for me."

"Name it," Mack said, already moving toward the door.

"Let me be the best man."

HOPE HAD NO idea where the men had taken her because as soon as she'd been pushed into the van, they'd tied a blindfold around her eyes and shoved her down on the floor. She'd hit her head hard.

She felt her attacker grab the strap of her crossover purse and yank it over her head and down her arm. Then the van had taken off fast. She'd spread her hands and tried to keep from bouncing around too much. She felt sick to her stomach and so terribly frightened that it was hard to keep from crying out.

But she kept still. And tried to listen to what the men were saying to one another. But it was useless. They were speaking in a language that she didn't understand.

She heard what sounded like a zipper and then the rush of wind as a window was lowered. One of the men said something, the other laughed and the window was shut.

Had something been tossed out the window? Her purse? Something else?

She did not think her capture had been random. The man had been waiting for her to come around the corner. He'd clapped his hand over her mouth and within seconds, she'd been inside the van. The van had been ready for her.

There must have been a woman. She'd asked about a woman, mid-forties with short brown hair, just the way Sasha had described her. The clerk had told her that there was a woman in the restroom.

Sasha was mid-forties with short brown hair.

Hope hadn't been scheduled to work. She'd only worked because Sasha had called her.

She felt sick. Had her friend betrayed her?

What did these men want? Ransom? Her parents would pay, she was sure of that.

Oh, God. Mack. He would be crazy with worry.

Their baby. Oh, please let their baby survive.

MACK AND BRODY caught a taxi outside the White House. From there, Mack called the pilot who had flown him in, and told him to get the plane ready, that he and Brody would be there in fifteen minutes to take off.

It was the longest fifteen minutes of Mack's life. He tried Hope's home number twice more. He didn't bother leaving messages.

The next call he made was to Chief Anderson. When the man answered, he sounded sleepy.

"Yes," he said.

"This is Mack McCann. I couldn't reach Hope and I had her cell phone tracked. It's in some kind of field next to Highway 52. She's in trouble. I need you to get somebody to her home and see if anyone is there."

"But, but…" the man sputtered. Then he sighed. "I'll go myself. I live pretty close to the Minnows." He hung up.

The cab stopped and Mack threw some money at the driver. He and Brody hit the pavement at a hard run. They boarded the plane, the pilot finished his take-off routine, and they were in the air in less than three minutes.

"It's going to be okay," Brody said.

Mack nodded. "It has to be." It had never mattered more.

Hope tried to keep track of the distance they were traveling by counting in her head. One, one thousand, two, one thousand, three, one thousand, all the way up to sixty, one thousand. She got through five full rounds and was halfway through a sixth before the van came to a pretty sudden stop. She heard doors opening.

She wasn't sure of the speed, but she thought it was likely within the speed limit, to not attract attention. That meant they were roughly five or six miles from the gas station where she'd been abducted.

It didn't tell her much but it did tell her something. She tried to listen for background noise. Was that a train in the distance? There were a couple of rail tracks, both freight and passenger, that ran through Weatherbie. Most were on the north end.

"Let's go." A hand gripped her upper arm and yanked her up. With her eyes still blindfolded, she missed a step and fell onto the ground.

Grass. Long grass.

The hand yanked her up again. They walked for just a minute and she heard a door open. Then she felt a temperature change as they entered a hot, stuffy building. A strong hand on her shoulder pushed her down onto a chair.

Finally, somebody ripped off her blindfold and she was looking at her abductors.

And she didn't have a clue who they were. Two men. Both with olive-colored skin and dark hair. Probably in their late thirties or early forties. One wore jeans and a white T-shirt. The other had on khaki pants and a long-sleeved dress shirt.

Most importantly, both had guns in their hands. It was hard to focus on anything but that. She forced herself to look back at the men's faces.

There was something about the man wearing the khaki pants.

The roundness of his face. The broad forehead.

And suddenly she remembered. The strip of photos in Sasha's car. The date for her cousin's wedding. It was definitely him.

More proof that Sasha was involved.

She swallowed, terribly afraid that she was going to throw up. Why would her friend do this?

She shifted her gaze, not wanting the man to see any flare of recognition in her eyes. The building was a metal structure with a cement floor. There was an old tractor and a hayrack stored at one end. Where they'd placed her, they had a cheap patio table with four chairs. There was a small refrigerator, the kind she'd had in college, near the table, with an extension cord running across the room to a wall outlet.

"Who are you?" Hope asked.

Neither man answered. The one in jeans opened the refrigerator and pulled out a beer. He tossed it to the other man and then pulled out a second one for himself.

"What do you want?" she asked.

"Shut up," Jeans-man said, this time in English.

When she heard his voice, she realized that was who had spoken to her in the van. Khaki-guy must have been driving. That meant that the keys were likely in his pocket.

The minute she got the chance, she was going for the keys and getting the heck out of here. But when Jeans-man suddenly put down his beer and grabbed a rope that was hanging on the wall, she knew her chances for escape had gotten much slimmer.

Chapter Twenty-Two

Mack and Brody touched down at the small private airstrip outside Weatherbie at exactly 8:00 p.m. Two minutes later, as they were driving toward the Minnow home, Mack got the call he'd been waiting for.

"I'm here at the Minnow house," Chief Anderson said. "Mavis got home about twenty minutes ago. There was no sign of Hope. Her car is gone. So is her purse. No sign of struggle. Mavis said the alarm was set when she let herself in."

"No note? No explanation?"

"No. I asked her and I checked myself. I didn't see anything."

There was no need for him to go to the house. He plugged the address that Pam Brogan had given him into his GPS. Then he repeated it to Chief Anderson, and added, "I'm headed there now. Meet me."

There was very little traffic and it took eight minutes to get there. It was on the outskirts of Weatherbie, where the pretty community started to turn more rural. There was a McDonald's on one corner, a gas station on another, a church with a big parking lot on the third corner and the fourth was still an empty field with a For Sale sign posted on it.

"That's got to be it," Brody said.

"Yeah." Mack parked and the men got out. They stood at the edge of the foot-high grass. It was going to be like looking for a needle in a haystack. Except not really. He dialed Hope's cell phone. Then he listened. Nothing. They separated, each man frantically redialing her number, hoping to hear a ring from somewhere. They were losing the daylight.

It took ten minutes before Brody called out. "I've got it."

Mack ran to his friend, crashing through the tall grass. There it was, sort of lying on top of the long grass. Like it would have been if someone had tossed it from the road.

None of the grass in the area was beaten down or showed any damage, except the paths that Brody and Mack had taken. He was sure that neither Hope nor her captor had actually been in the field.

Out of the corner of his eye, he saw flashing blue lights and knew that Chief Anderson had arrived. There were two squad cars with him.

The chief and the two other officers walked into the field. Mack nodded at the men. "This is my friend, Brody Donovan." Then he pointed to Hope's phone. "I'm sure it's Hope's, but I haven't touched it yet. I don't have any gloves."

One of the officers snapped on a pair and reached for the phone. "We need to check her calls," Mack said.

The chief nodded and the officer pressed a button. He showed Mack the screen. She hadn't made any calls that day. The only incoming calls were the ones he'd made in D.C. and the thirty or forty calls that he and Brody had made in the last few minutes.

"Check the texts," he said next.

There was his text from D.C. Nothing else. Damn it. He turned to the chief. "Hope was near here. I don't

know why, but she was. We need to question everyone in
the area. I think the lowest possibility is the church. There
are no cars in the parking lot and quite frankly, if she
drove somewhere, I don't think it was to visit an empty
church. But she could have run to get gas or to pick up
some food, although I've yet to see her eat any fast food."

Chief Anderson pointed to one of the officers. "Check
the church." He pointed to the other. "You go with Brody
and check McDonald's. Mack and I'll take Smart Gas.
Switch your radios to channel two for secure communication."

"Wait," Mack said. He pulled his cell phone out of
his shirt pocket, opened up his pictures and found one
of Hope. "Here's Hope's picture," he said, holding it out
so the men could have a good look. Then he looked at
his friend. "I'll forward it to your phone so that you can
show people."

"Got it," Brody said. Then he looked at Mack. "We're
going to find her."

Mack didn't answer. He had a horrible feeling that
time was not their friend.

When he and Chief Anderson went into the gas station, there was one clerk and three people waiting to get
checked out. The chief pulled his badge, said "excuse
me" a couple times and they were suddenly at the front of
the line. In the meantime, Mack had checked each aisle.

"Good luck," said the male clerk to the customer who
had just bought a lottery ticket.

They needed all the luck right now. He and Chief Anderson stepped close to the counter.

The chief flashed his badge again. "My name is Chief
Anderson from the Weatherbie Police Department. We're

looking for this woman." He motioned for Mack to hold out his phone.

The man looked at it. "Pretty. She do something wrong?"

"She's...missing," the chief said.

Mack hated hearing that word. *Missing.* "Have you seen her?"

"I just came on about a half hour ago. Hank would have been working the register before that, but he's gone for the day."

Damn. "Do you have a security camera?" Mack asked.

The man frowned at him. "Of course."

"We need to see it," Mack said. "Everything from this evening."

"You'll have to talk to my manager, Tammy, for that."

Mack leaned his face in close. "Get Tammy out here. Now."

JEANS-MAN HAD PULLED her hands behind her back, led her over to a wooden stake that she suspected had been installed just for her and tied her to it. Then he and Khaki-guy had left the building.

Her shoulders burned, her head hurt from where she'd hit it on the van floor, but the pain in her heart was the worst.

Sasha had been a trusted confidante when Hope had first come to Gloria's Path. She'd helped Hope have the courage to leave Wills and, ultimately, the resolve to come back and volunteer. They were friends.

At least she'd thought they were.

She'd thought that there could never be a betrayal that would be as horrible or as painful as when her father had chosen Wills over her. But this somehow felt worse.

Her father had been motivated by his greed for fame and money. While she detested that, she understood it.

What had Sasha's motivation been?

It didn't matter, Hope realized. All that mattered is that she had to stay alive. Whatever it took, whatever she ultimately had to endure.

She owed that to herself, to Mack and most of all, to the child that she carried in her womb. Mack would come back, he'd see the note on the calendar on the refrigerator and he'd start to put the pieces together. He would find her. If anyone could. And she was going to be alive when he did.

TAMMY BURDEN WAS barely five feet tall, but she carried herself like a woman who tolerated very little bull. Chief Anderson introduced himself and Mack before quickly and quietly explaining the situation.

Tammy stared at them. "Hope Minnow was my tennis partner in high school. Oh, good Lord. You're the sexy stranger that Jane was Tweeting about."

Mack nodded.

Tammy shook her head. "Jane never did have any common sense. Come on. Let's go take a look."

The quality of the security camera video was not great, but certainly better than some he'd worked with. Plus, it wasn't like he was trying to pick someone out of a lineup. He was looking for the woman he loved. And he found her easily enough.

"There she is," he said. He checked the time on the tape—6:14 p.m. Almost two hours ago now. "She's talking to your clerk." He tried to read her lips. "Meet a woman." He got that much. The clerk was pointing toward something. What the hell was he pointing at?

Tammy was already picking up the phone. She dialed,

then spoke. "Hank, it's Tammy. Sorry to bother you but I have a quick question. About a half hour before your shift ended, a pretty blond woman came in. She spoke to you, maybe asked you something about meeting a woman and you pointed outside. Do you remember that?"

Mack wanted to jerk the phone out of her hand, to demand to talk to Hank, but Tammy had been pretty helpful so far. He didn't want to push his luck. He looked at Chief Anderson and got the impression that he was thinking the same thing.

"Okay, thanks," Tammy said and hung up her phone. "Hank definitely remembers Hope. Said she had come in, looked around, then asked whether there was a brown-haired woman in her mid-forties in the store. He told her that he'd just given the restroom key to someone who fit that description. He said that he assumed that she went to find her. He was mad because nobody ever came back in with the key. When his shift was over, he went out to check and the key was on the bathroom floor. He hung it back up." She pointed to a key with a foot-long metal rod for a handle. It was hanging on the wall behind the clerk's head.

"Don't touch that key again. Don't give it to anybody. Don't let anybody use that restroom," Chief Anderson instructed. He spoke into the radio that was on his lapel. "Report to Smart Gas. Repeat, report to Smart Gas."

He looked at Mack. "I'll get my two officers back here to process the scene."

"Is there a security camera by the restrooms?" Mack asked.

"I'm sorry, but not on that side of the building."

"On your pumps?" he persisted.

"Of course. You think she got gas?"

He doubted that. There were two possibilities. One, the

brown-haired woman was in as much trouble as Hope. Two, the brown-haired woman had been a ruse and someone accosted Hope on her way to the ladies room. They'd driven off with her. Maybe they would get lucky and at least get some sort of vehicle description. "I want to see everything from six o'clock to about six-twenty."

Tammy quickly typed in some commands on her desktop and soon she was showing a view of the pump area. There were three pumps, with cars pulling up on both sides. They watched. Nothing seemed unusual. Until Mack saw the blue work van. It passed by the far end of the pumps, but the driver, middle-aged, wearing a ball cap low on his forehead, didn't pull in to fill up his tank.

They lost him from the screen. "Where did he go?" Mack asked. "Where the hell did he go?"

"Maybe he pulled in to turn around," Tammy said. "That happens a lot out here. People looking for stuff in Weatherbie and suddenly realizing that they're getting out of the city limits."

There was no way to know because the camera did not provide a view of the entryway off the street. "Go back to the other camera," Mack said. "See if he came inside to buy something."

They looked. No men in baseball caps entered. In fact, no men at all entered.

Mack made eye contact with the chief. The older man nodded. Then he spoke into his radio, asking for all officers to be aware of a blue van with a dent on the right rear fender panel. Once he finished, he made eye contact. "Okay. That will get communicated statewide."

Tammy looked at the two men. "I'm sorry," she said. "I wish we had more for you, but nothing bad ever happens in Weatherbie."

Mack knew that bad stuff happened everywhere. And

sometimes it was random. But that wasn't the case here. Hope had come looking for someone. But who? And who had sent her on the wild-goose chase? If he could figure that out, he would find her.

"I think we've done what we can do," Chief Anderson said. "I suggest you go back to the Minnows' place and hopefully, we'll get a demand call. I'm going to contact the FBI and ask for some assistance."

Mack looked at his watch. The Minnows were due to land at JFK International Airport in New York in less than two hours. It was going to be impossible to keep a lid on the fact that the missing woman was Hope Minnow. He could not let them hear this news from anyone but him.

Hope had been his responsibility and he'd failed her.

The only thing worse than that was the possibility that he'd lost her forever.

Chapter Twenty-Three

Hope wasn't sure how long the men left her alone in the shed, but she thought it was several hours. She was tired of standing, her throat was raw from screaming, her shoulders and back ached terribly from the awkward position of having her hands tied behind her back and she desperately needed to use the bathroom.

But it was the feeling of isolation, of being so very alone, that was the worst. What if no one ever came back? What if they had left her here to die? How long would it take? Days? A week before her body started to shut down from lack of water, lack of nutrients? It was a horrible thought. And it played with her mind.

When the door finally opened, she was almost grateful to see the faces of her kidnappers. They looked at her, little emotion on their faces. Khaki-guy with the buffed fingernails had changed his shirt. It was still long-sleeved but now blue instead of a gray-and-white stripe. His hair looked cleaner, too.

Had he showered and changed clothes? The fact that he could do something so mundane after kidnapping someone made her stomach roll. Had he gone to Sasha's house?

She made eye contact with him. "I need to use the restroom. Badly."

He seemed to hesitate. Then he walked over and untied her. She rolled her shoulders forward, praying that she wouldn't pass out when the tendons and ligaments protested. He grabbed her upper arm tightly.

"Don't do anything stupid," he said. He led her to the door that he and Jeans-man had been using. He opened it and Hope could see that it was a small office area. There was a television on the wall showing a soccer game. Remnants of the fast-food dinner the two men had consumed were still on the desk. Her stomach rumbled loudly.

He ignored it and pointed toward the bathroom. "If you're not out in a minute, I'm coming in."

The bathroom was small with just a toilet and a sink. If the man had showered, he'd done it somewhere else. Maybe when he'd picked up the food. She hadn't heard the van start or return but she believed that at least one of them had left.

Would they do that again? It would be easier to fight one than two. She would use every bit of her strength, her teeth, whatever it took.

Hope used the toilet and tried to find something that she could use as a weapon. But there was nothing. No hairspray, no razors, no nothing. Just a bar of soap and some paper towels.

She flushed, washed her hands and opened the door. Khaki-guy was watching the television.

"What do you want?" she asked. "It's not too late to fix this."

He just looked at her. "Let's go," he said.

"May I have something to drink?" she asked, trying to sound submissive, nonthreatening.

He didn't answer. Just led her back into the big room. On their way past the refrigerator, he grabbed her a bottle of water. He watched as she opened it and took a big drink.

She heard his phone buzz and he reached into his khaki pants and pulled it out. He looked at the screen, then looked at Jeans-man. "It's starting," he said. "Won't be long now."

Jeans-man nodded several times, as if he were nervous.

What was starting?

He pulled the half-drunk bottle of water away from her. "That's enough."

Then he led her back to the pole and tied her up again.

MACK USED HIS connections to get through airport security so that he could be waiting at the gate when the plane landed. Now he waited, pacing back and forth.

He'd called Mavis from the car. The woman had been calm, certainly calmer than he felt. He'd told her to expect the police and the FBI to arrive shortly. "I'll be here," she'd told him.

He saw Bing first. Then Patsy Minnow, with Archie Minnow bringing up the rear. They all looked tired.

"Mack?" Bing said, slightly apprehensive. Nobody met travelers at the gate anymore.

Mack's throat almost closed with emotion, and he shook his head. "I'm sorry," he said. Then he turned to Patsy and Archie. "Hope went missing tonight, approximately six hours ago. The local police and the FBI have been alerted. So far, we have not received a ransom demand."

Patsy let out a soft squeal, like a wounded puppy might make. Archie's face lost all color. Bing's dark eyes drilled him.

"But that awful man was caught," Patsy said. He could hear her bewilderment.

"It's someone else," Mack said. He wanted to swear

to them that he'd figure it out, bring Hope home, but he had nothing, absolutely nothing, to go on. "Mavis is at the house. I know she's anxious to be with both of you."

But before they were out of the airport, Mack's phone rang. He yanked it out of his pocket. *Brody.* "What do we know?" he answered.

- "We got a call," Brody said. "They made a ransom demand. Five million dollars. By noon tomorrow."

"Proof of life? Did you get it?" Mack demanded.

"We did. Hope's alive. They told her to say something and she said, 'Tell Mack that I loved the north donuts.'"

Loved the north donuts. What the hell? "You're sure that's what she said?"

"I heard it myself. We had it on speakerphone."

North as in a company name? Donuts? He'd never bought her donuts from North Donuts or any other donut shop. They'd never even talked about donuts.

Except they had. She'd been talking about a story that she'd heard about an old guy in a nursing home who escaped, naked, to buy his elderly girlfriend a donut.

She was being held at a nursing home? A nursing home called North.

No. That didn't make sense. Near a nursing home? On the north side of town? Maybe.

Held by someone who was old?

Held by someone who worked at a nursing home? Held by the person who told the story?

Sasha.

He stepped away from the rest of the group. "Brody, I need you to do something, but don't say anything to anyone else." He didn't know whom he could trust. "I think the woman that Hope worked with at Gloria's Path, one of the paid staff, is involved. Her first name is Sasha.

Don't know the last name or her address, but I'm betting we can get it from somebody at that shelter."

"I'm on it," Brody said.

They exited the airport. It was a quiet ride back to the Minnows' house. Everyone seemed lost in their own thoughts.

The only thing Reverend Minnow said was that he intended to pay. He would go to his bank in the morning.

Mack was grateful that the man wasn't balking at the request. He could have come up with a sizable portion himself, but it would have taken him a few days to raise the rest. Time they might not have.

They might not have it anyway, he knew. Kidnapping cases rarely ended well, even when the ransom demands were met. Kidnappers got nervous and killed the victim, sometimes before they got the money, sometimes immediately after.

But for now, Hope was alive. At least she had been fifteen minutes earlier.

They turned down the long driveway and parked behind several police cars. When they entered the house, at least six agents and several more officers in uniforms looked up. Mavis had made coffee and there was a big plate of cookies on the counter.

It could have been a damn party except that everybody looked very serious.

"Local press was here," Chief Anderson said, pulling him aside. "No one, of course, said anything about a ransom demand, but I still think it's going to get big play, especially after what happened last week to Hope."

Publicity. It was what Hope hated the most. She'd been so convinced that the threats against her were a publicity stunt. Was it possible that she was right? Was her father so hungry for press coverage that he'd do something like this?

Mack approached Reverend Minnow, who appeared to have aged ten years since he'd gotten off the plane. But Mack wasn't about to let that stop him. "May I speak with you privately?" he asked.

Archie Minnow nodded. "Of course." He led him to the library and closed the French doors.

Mack didn't waste any time. "I know that you and your daughter have a strained relationship. I also know that William Baylor beat the hell out of her and that for some crazy reason, you continue to employ him."

Archie pursed his lips, but didn't say anything.

"Hope initially dismissed the threats against her because she believed that it might be a publicity stunt to push your book sales. But the threats were real and Wayne Smother was real. We thought it was over. But now this. I'm going to ask just once. Are you involved in this in any way?" He expected the man to bristle but he didn't.

Archie merely shook his head. "I made a mistake with William. He was like a son to me, long before he married Hope. I liked him. Hell, I loved him. And I knew that I would not have achieved the success I had without his help. He's really very brilliant. Seemed to know exactly the right steps for me to take. And when the two of them started having trouble, I got scared. I thought I'd fail if William wasn't part of my team, and I'd worked my whole damn life to get where I was."

Mack really wanted to slam a fist in the man's mouth. But he kept silent.

"I was surprised when Hope told me what had happened. And I saw her injuries. They were bad. I talked to William about it. His story was different. I wasn't there,

I told myself. How could I know? What I did know for sure was that if the story got out, it would be bad for the ministry. Everyone knew that William was my right-hand man, my hand-picked successor, in fact."

"Hope believes you chose William over her."

"I know that. She's wrong, you know," he said, his voice thick with emotion. "I did something worse. And I have regretted it for a very long time. I can't expect her to forgive me. You see, I chose myself over her. And that's not what a parent is supposed to do. Parents put the needs of their children first. I didn't do that. I'm not proud of what I did. And ultimately, I'll be judged by my god and I can only pray for His forgiveness. I've already told her mother the truth. I did it after you called us in Paris. We almost lost Hope. I knew I finally needed to be honest with Patsy."

"And what did she say?"

"She was upset, of course. But I think she understands. Patsy has always understood how important the ministry was to me. It's important to her, too." The man cleared his throat, then looked toward the doors, as if checking to make sure they were still shut. "You need to know something. The two threats that we received, those letters, Patsy leaked the information to Byron Ferguson. And told him that Hope had a bodyguard. That's where he got his information."

Of all the things that Mack had expected to hear, this wasn't one of them. "Why?"

"In the past, I've gotten strange letters from parishioners and followers. Some are very zealous about their faith. While these were different, Patsy told me that she didn't really believe that Hope was in danger, especially with you around. She thought the publicity would be good for book sales. She did it for me."

Mack thought his head might burst. "I want you to know something. I love your daughter. Very much. And she loves me." He drew in a deep breath. "I'm going to marry her."

Archie Minnow stared at him. Finally, he spoke. "Although you may not believe it, I really am a very spiritual man. I am praying for Hope. I'm praying for all of us."

"I'm going to find her," Mack said. "If it's the last thing I do."

MACK RETURNED TO the kitchen. With the ransom demand in, everyone was mainly in wait-and-see mode. Agents were talking quietly in small groups. Someone had brought in pizza and the aroma filled the small kitchen.

Mavis was at the far counter. She was wearing the same shirt as the morning when she'd come in with it buttoned wrong. The morning she'd been reluctant to leave Hope and Mack alone. The morning she'd gone through the calendar with them.

He looked at the wall.

The calendar was already showing tomorrow's date.

That wasn't right. Mavis tore off the previous day's sheet every morning. He'd seen her. Sure, it was possible that someone else had changed the date. But how likely was that?

Not very. The calendar was Mavis's domain.

If Mavis had done it early by chance, then she'd likely thrown it away in the garbage. Old habits were hard to break.

Casually, he pulled a paper napkin out of the dispenser and spit out the piece of gum he was chewing into it. He folded it up, walked over to the sink and opened the cupboard door that was below the sink. He tossed in the napkin.

To an empty garbage can. Absolutely empty.

He distinctly remembered emptying coffee grounds into that garbage can just that morning. Somebody had taken the garbage out. In the middle of a crisis?

He shut the door and poured himself a glass of water. Drank it, standing at the sink. Nobody was paying any attention to him. Mavis had moved into the living room and sat next to Hope's mother, talking quietly to her.

He walked outside to the veranda. It was a warm night and he stood, watching the pool. Anyone watching him would think that he was gathering his thoughts.

After a minute, he moved to the corner of the house, toward the garbage cans that lined the side of the garage. He lifted the lid and pulled out the plastic bag on top. He opened the bag and used the flashlight on his key ring to look at the contents.

Amidst coffee grounds, leftover spaghetti, and newspapers, he found what he was looking for. He unfolded the ball of paper and smoothed it out.

Ran to the store—needed cornstarch. Will be back in a little while. That was in Mavis's handwriting.

Need to help a client. Eat without me and I'll grab something when I get home. Hope's reply.

Mavis had deliberately withheld this information. Why would she do that?

The only possible explanation was that Mavis was in this up to her eyeballs.

Chapter Twenty-Four

He pulled out his phone to call Brody. "Where are you?"

"Just left Gloria's Path. The woman is Sasha Roher, and I have her address."

"From who?"

"From nobody. There was nobody in the lobby area. It's still damaged from the fire. They haven't started re-building. But they also haven't cleared out any of their paperwork. It was still in the steel filing cabinet. I managed to get it open and there were tax forms for all the employees. There was only one Sasha. I'm on my way to her house now."

"Swing by and pick me up," Mack said. "I'll be waiting for you at the end of the lane." He didn't intend to announce to anybody that he was leaving.

Brody pulled up in Mack's car a couple minutes later. He got out so that Mack could drive. When Mack told him about the calendar page in the garbage, his friend hissed through his teeth.

Exactly.

He put Sasha Roher's address into his GPS and took off fast. They were at their destination in less than ten minutes. It was a small-frame house, maybe a two-bedroom. There was a narrow driveway that led to the garage, which backed up to the alley. The garage door was down. There was a light on in the back of the house.

"Take the back door," Mack said. "I'm going in through the front."

He walked up the three front steps, opened the screen door and turned the knob of the front door. Locked. He could hear music playing, something loud with a lot of drums. Finally, something was going his way.

He lifted his leg and kicked the door handle. Two quick kicks and the wood frame splintered. He pushed through the door. The house smelled like cinnamon. He glanced into the kitchen. Clean, nothing out of place. Same with the small living room. Nothing to make him think that any violence had occurred here. That made him feel only slightly better.

He passed the bathroom as he walked down the hall. He stuck his head around the corner of the room where the light was on. Sasha had her back to him. She was dancing to the beat of the music while she packed a suitcase on her unmade bed. There was also an open purse on the bed. In it, a small handgun.

He put his gun against her temple and wrapped an arm around her neck.

She tried to jump but couldn't budge him. "Going somewhere?" he asked, his mouth close to her ear.

"How did you get in?" she asked, her voice trembling.

Good. He wanted her scared. "I'm going to give you three seconds to tell me where Hope Minnow is. If you don't, I'm going to shoot you. One. Two." He took a breath. Opened his mouth.

"How would I know?" she asked, trying to act tough.

He took a chance. "Because you picked a partner who doesn't stand up to questioning very well. Mavis may look tough but she's a cupcake. She rolled over on you like a dog wanting his belly scratched."

He could feel the air leave the woman's body. "Damn it," she said.

"The only way for you to help yourself now is to tell me where Hope is."

"I don't know where she is."

The woman was lying. He pulled out his cell phone and dialed Brody. When he answered, he spoke fast. "Officer Donovan," he said. "I need you to contact Officer Ethan Moore. Tell him that Ms. Roher resisted arrest and I was forced to shoot her in self-defense."

He held the phone away from his ear so that Sasha could hear Brody's response.

"Roger that," Brody said. "I'll call the coroner, too."

He shoved Sasha away from him, spinning her so that she faced him. There was less than three feet that separated them.

"Goodbye, Sasha," he said. He pointed his gun at her heart.

"Wait," she cried. "They have her in an old machine shed. Off County Road C where it crosses Route 126."

That was north of town. "Who?" Mack demanded.

"My boyfriend and his brother. But this was all Mavis's idea. She's the one who thought up this crazy scheme. She told my boyfriend that it would work."

"How does she know your boyfriend?"

"He's her younger brother."

Mack dialed Brody. "Get in here. Use the front door."

When Brody walked into the bedroom, Mack smiled at him. "Roger that?"

Brody shrugged. "I don't get the chance to watch many police dramas."

Mack nodded at the open purse. "Get that gun and make sure it's loaded."

Brody knew his way around guns. As kids, they'd hunted in the mountains and Brody always had a good shot. Steady hands that served him well as a surgeon.

"It's loaded. Six bullets."

"Take a test shot. Make sure it shoots."

Brody put a round into the headboard. "Fires a hair to the right. I can correct for that."

"I'm counting on that. Keep your gun on her. Don't hesitate to shoot if she tries anything. I'm going to call Chief Anderson and they'll be here to back you up within a couple minutes."

"Where are you going?" Brody asked.

"I'm going to go find the woman I love. When the cops get here, you can tell them that they'll find me at the corner of County C Road and Route 126."

"You don't want to wait?" Brody asked.

"Hell, no," Mack said and left the house.

He wasn't going to take a chance that the cavalry would descend upon the machine shed and Hope would get caught in the crossfire. He was going in quiet.

He drove fast and arrived seven minutes later. He parked his car a half mile away and ran the rest of the distance. He wasn't even breathing hard when he got there.

When he saw the blue van outside of the building, his heart started beating a little fast. He walked around the building. Two doors. One was a regular house door. The other at the rear of the building was a garage door big enough to pull machinery in and out.

There were three windows on each side, but way too high to be useful to him. He was going to have to go through the front door. He needed to figure out a way to make them open the door without making them suspicious that they were under attack.

He looked around and considered his options. He studied the van. It might work. There was a patch of grass between the front of the van and the building, maybe three feet wide. Just a little downward slope. Maybe enough.

He opened the door of the van, hoping that the idiots had left the keys inside. They hadn't.

Okay. Plan B. He got out, got flat on his back and moved underneath the van. Using his flashlight, he carefully located the cable running alongside the transmission that had a switch and lever connected to it. He disconnected the cable and pushed on the lever until it clicked twice. The van moved forward just a little, telling him he had managed to get it in Neutral.

He crawled out. Then he braced his back against the rear of the van and pushed like hell until the thing started rolling forward. Then he ran.

He rounded the corner of the machine shed just as the van hit the building. It wasn't going fast enough to go through, but it dented the side of the building and made a hell of a noise.

That's what he'd been counting on.

The door opened and a man stuck his head out, looking around. He had a flashlight. "What the hell?" he said, when he saw the van. He shined the light around a little more and was evidently satisfied when he didn't see any other vehicles. He walked out, leaving the door open behind him.

Mack let him get close to the van before he walked up behind him and knocked him in the head with his gun. The man crumpled to the ground. Mack opened the van door, dragged the man inside and used a rope he found in the back to tie the man's hands behind his back. Then he backed out of the van, flipping the door locks to lock the man in.

He walked through the door of the machine shed, into a small office area. There was a television going in the corner and a half-empty beer on the old metal desk.

He opened the door that connected the office to the back part of the machine shed. The door creaked and he moved fast, knowing that he'd lost the element of surprise.

But he didn't move fast enough. He saw Hope, then the second man just as they saw him.

The man, who had been untying Hope's hands, grabbed her and pulled her in front of him, taking his shot away.

His heart plummeted. He'd come so far, he could not lose her now.

Then he saw Hope knot her hands together, raise them over her shoulder and knock the man hard enough in his larynx that he stumbled back.

It was all Mack needed.

By the time the man recovered, Mack had his gun pointed at the man's chest.

And he heard the sounds of approaching sirens.

THIRTY MINUTES LATER, Mack was sitting on the grass, with his back against the machine shed, Hope in his arms. The cool night air felt good.

"I knew you would come," she said.

"You were so smart," he said, kissing her forehead. She was alive. "I wouldn't have got it without the donut clue."

When he'd called Chief Anderson after leaving Sasha's house, he'd given the man a quick rundown of what was going on. The man had agreed to contain Mavis and

send backup for Brody. He'd told Mack, in no uncertain
terms, to do nothing else, to leave it to the police.

So the man had been a little irritated after he'd gotten the address from Brody to find that Mack had one
suspect tied up in the van and the other held at gunpoint.
But he'd rallied quickly and spent a little of the last half
hour filling them in.

When the chief had confronted Mavis, she initially
denied any role in Hope's disappearance. Then, when
Reverend Minnow asked her to please tell them the truth,
she'd broken down. Had admitted that she'd overheard
Patsy on the telephone, leaking information to Byron Ferguson about the threats. Had thought that if something
bad actually happened to Hope, that it would all come
out and that Archie would be so angry with his wife that
he would turn to her for solace.

"She admitted," the chief had said, "in front of a whole
room of people that she was in love with Reverend Minnow, that she'd been in love with him since she and Patsy
were sorority sisters and Archie had chosen Patsy over
her."

Mavis had sought help from her brother, who recently
started dating Sasha Roher, and they devised a plan to
kidnap Hope. It was supposed to happen after the Minnows were home and Mack was gone. When Mavis had
learned that Mack was out of town for the evening, she'd
put the plan in play.

"I thought Sasha was my friend," Hope said, sounding sad. "And Mavis? She's been living in our home all
this time."

"She was jealous of your mother. Had been for years. I
guess that kind of emotion can wear a person down after
a while and make them do crazy things."

"I recognized the man when I saw him. I knew it was

the man in the pictures with Sasha. And I kept thinking there was something else very familiar about him. I guess I was seeing the resemblance to Mavis."

"He enlisted the help of his brother-in-law. It was a regular family affair. Maybe they can all get cells close together." He stroked her hair. "By the way, you gave that guy a pretty good shot in there, with your hands clasped together like that."

She smiled. "I wonder if I should call Wills and thank him."

"Huh?"

"I felt very vulnerable after what had happened with Wills. It led me to six months of self-defense training. That was one of the moves our instructor showed us. Guess it goes to show that a little good comes out of everything."

"I don't think you're going to have to worry much about running into your ex. Something tells me he's not going to be working at the ministry much longer."

"You know something I don't know?" she asked.

He shrugged. "I think you need to talk to your parents."

"I do. I want to see them. I...have a lot to tell them," Hope said.

"I'll be right there with you," he said.

"There's something I should tell you first," Hope said, turning in his arms to face him.

"Okay."

"I got offered the job in Brooklyn."

He smiled. "That's good news, right?" He could live in Brooklyn. He could live anywhere that Hope was.

"I turned it down."

"Why?"

"There's something else I have to tell you."

He waited.

"I'm pregnant."

He could feel the blood in his veins pumping. "How do you know?"

"I took a pregnancy test. Two of them, in fact. I am definitely pregnant."

Now his heart was swelling in his chest. Pregnant. He was going to be a father.

"And I have something else I need to tell you," she said.

"My head is starting to whirl, darlin'," he said.

"Yes."

"Yes, what?"

"Yes, I will marry you. I love you. I trust you. I know that I'm not making a mistake. I want to live in Colorado with you. I want to see those cabins that you've talked about. I want our child to see them."

Mack leaned close and kissed her. Softly. Then he stood up and held out his hand for her. "And I want to tell our child about the day I fell in love with Hope Minnow, aka Hopeless Fish Bait. A woman so beautiful, so kind and so amazingly brave, who has made me the happiest man ever."

* * * * *

THE MEN OF CROW HOLLOW *comes to an
exciting conclusion next month.
Look for Beverly Long's TRAPPED
wherever Harlequin Intrigue books are sold!*

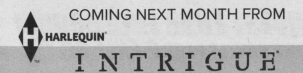

COMING NEXT MONTH FROM

HARLEQUIN®

INTRIGUE®

Available September 16, 2014

HICNM0914

REQUEST YOUR FREE BOOKS!
2 FREE NOVELS PLUS 2 FREE GIFTS!

⬧HARLEQUIN®

INTRIGUE®

BREATHTAKING ROMANTIC SUSPENSE

YES! Please send me 2 FREE Harlequin Intrigue® novels and my 2 FREE gifts (gifts are worth about $10). After receiving them, if I don't wish to receive any more books, I can return the shipping statement marked "cancel." If I don't cancel, I will receive 6 brand-new novels every month and be billed just $4.74 per book in the U.S. or $5.24 per book in Canada. That's a savings of at least 14% off the cover price! It's quite a bargain! Shipping and handling is just 50¢ per book in the U.S. and 75¢ per book in Canada.* I understand that accepting the 2 free books and gifts places me under no obligation to buy anything. I can always return a shipment and cancel at any time. Even if I never buy another book, the two free books and gifts are mine to keep forever.

182/382 HDN F42N

Name _____ (PLEASE PRINT)

Address _____ Apt. #

City _____ State/Prov. _____ Zip/Postal Code

Signature (if under 18, a parent or guardian must sign)

Mail to the **Harlequin® Reader Service:**
IN U.S.A.: P.O. Box 1867, Buffalo, NY 14240-1867
IN CANADA: P.O. Box 609, Fort Erie, Ontario L2A 5X3
Are you a subscriber to Harlequin Intrigue books
and want to receive the larger-print edition?
Call 1-800-873-8635 or visit www.ReaderService.com.

* Terms and prices subject to change without notice. Prices do not include applicable taxes. Sales tax applicable in N.Y. Canadian residents will be charged applicable taxes. Offer not valid in Quebec. This offer is limited to one order per household. Not valid for current subscribers to Harlequin Intrigue books. All orders subject to credit approval. Credit or debit balances in a customer's account(s) may be offset by any other outstanding balance owed by or to the customer. Please allow 4 to 6 weeks for delivery. Offer available while quantities last.

Your Privacy—The Harlequin® Reader Service is committed to protecting your privacy. Our Privacy Policy is available online at www.ReaderService.com or upon request from the Harlequin Reader Service.

We make a portion of our mailing list available to reputable third parties that offer products we believe may interest you. If you prefer that we not exchange your name with third parties, or if you wish to clarify or modify your communication preferences, please visit us at www.ReaderService.com/consumerchoice or write to us at Harlequin Reader Service Preference Service, P.O. Box 9062, Buffalo, NY 14269. Include your complete name and address.

HI13R

SPECIAL EXCERPT FROM

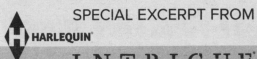

HARLEQUIN®

I N T R I G U E

*When a woman from his past shows up with newborn
twins and claims she needs his protection, a Texas
lawman will risk everything to keep them all safe…*

Read on for an excerpt from
COWBOY BEHIND THE BADGE
by USA TODAY *bestselling author*
Delores Fossen

Laine didn't push him away. A big surprise. But she
did look up at him. "Ironic, huh? When you woke up
yesterday morning, I'll bet you never thought we'd be
voluntarily touching each other."

Tucker shook his head, hoping it'd clear it. It didn't
work. Maybe he should try hitting it against the wall. "Who
says this is voluntary?"

A short burst of air left her mouth. Almost a laugh. Then
that troubled look returned to her eyes. "It's not a good idea
for us to be here alone."

"No. It's not."

There. They were in complete agreement. Still, neither
of them moved a muscle. Well, he moved some. His grip
tightened on her a little, and those kissing dreams returned
with a vengeance.

"Besides, I'm no longer your type," she added, as if that
would help.

It didn't.

However, it did cause him to temporarily scowl. "How

would you know my type?"

Another huff. Soft and silky, though, not rough like his. Her breath brushed against his mouth almost like a kiss. Almost. "Everyone in town knows. Blonde, busty and not looking for a commitment."

He was sure his scowl wasn't so brief that time, but the problem was he couldn't argue with her about it. Besides, the reminder accomplished what Laine had likely intended.

Tucker stepped back from her.

He figured that she'd say something smart-mouthed to keep things light, but she didn't. For a moment Laine actually looked a little disappointed that their little hugging session had ended, and that was all the more reason for him to not pick it up again.

Ever.

Even if parts of him were suggesting just that.

With killers hot on their trail and innocent babies in need of protection, a sizzling attraction should be the last thing on Tucker's and Laine's minds.

Find out how long they'll be able to contain it when the second book in USA TODAY *bestselling author Delores Fossen's* **SWEETWATER RANCH** *miniseries,* COWBOY BEHIND THE BADGE, *goes on sale in October 2014!*

INTRIGUE